COOKIE GIRL CHRISTMAS

CHRISTENE HOUSTON

For Emogene Houston who shed a
tear at the first carol of the season and
now watches over my little ones until they
are delivered to my arms. Until we meet,
my dear friend, thank you.

CHAPTER ONE

"Call out the Coast Guard, I think we're out of buttercream." I smoothed a strand of golden hair behind one ear, straightening my apron and searching the room in a careful review. Everything was in order despite the strain of panic running through my nerves that made each twinkle light shine more brightly.

Carefully, I listed things I was grateful for in my mind.

I'm grateful to work with my best friend, even if she's easily distracted.

I'm grateful for the magic of Christmas.

I'm grateful this job gets me one step closer to a shop of my own.

The tightness in my chest eased, and my shoulders sank an inch with each thought.

"You forget who you're working with. We not only have plenty of buttercream, but we also have extras of almost everything on the dessert table." Vee Devereaux, my lovely assistant, rolled her eyes at the typical case of nerves that often set in on demanding jobs. "I can drool over hot boys *and* get the job done all at once. It's why you hired me." Her smile was smug, the one she used when trying to diffuse the anxiety from the air.

When that didn't work, she sighed. "Molls, ya gotta relax. You're tensing up over nothing. These people already think you're amazing. I mean, they've hired you for the entire flippin' season. You're going to pay off the minivan in one fell swoop!"

I ducked behind her, scanning the room for Vanessa Davenport, the wealthy young mother who'd hired me. I shushed Vee with a whispered, "Genevieve, don't talk money at the party!"

"Really? I'm Genevieve now? In case you hadn't noticed, the party hasn't started yet. See, that guy is still slurping cocoa at the counter. Note to self, dark washed jeans look oh so good on a man."

I sighed, "Oh, Vee. I thought you and Jon were still an 'item'."

"Please, you know he's my one and only. I'm just picturing *his* bum in *those* jeans … it's a lovely thought."

I did my best to keep my imagination in check. The last thing I needed was an image of Vee's boyfriend in anything less than a snowsuit. Besides, I was too focused on making sure that things were perfect to be distracted by good fitting jeans. To be honest, I would never have noticed the jeans to begin with. I would have noticed the strong, broad shoulders and the admittedly sexy biceps straining at the sleeves of his shirt. Not that I was looking.

The Davenports were my best clients. An almost monthly stipend of cookie boxes supplemented their generous holiday extravaganza to friends, neighbors, and teachers—all gifts that originated from The Cookie Jar: my bakery and party planning business that promised to have its own store front by late next year. This holiday season, they brought it all up a notch by hiring me as their dessert caterer for an extended welcome home party. A long lost son was revisiting the family manor and reportedly was the cousin of Buddy the Elf in regard to his love of Christmas. Thus, the Twelve Days of Christmas was decided upon, with a new party every other night to extend the celebration throughout the month of December, beginning on the 3rd. I was in charge of the fancy cookies and beautifully arranged tables spread with holiday confections.

Genevieve Devereaux was my best friend and willing partner in these shenanigans. When there were cookies to be made or elaborate tables to be constructed, she was my go-to girl. Genevieve, or Vee as she preferred to be called, had an eye for style and a knack for seeing what I missed.

Besides, she was one person who really got me and my slightly manic drive for perfection. She didn't seem to mind that I spent so much time going over each cookie in precise detail. And she understood the constant whispered gratitudes that came out of my mouth when I was feeling stressed.

Like now, when the bloom of panic in my chest told me I had forgotten something important. I just didn't know what.

I'm grateful for Vee's superpower ability to catch my mistakes, even if she has an attitude about it.

"Handmade Santa face cookies, white and green chocolate dipped berries, white chocolate popcorn in paper cones, red and green jelly beans …" I ticked off the items on my mental checklist as I looked them over. The table was Christmas joy on display, decked in reds and green with gold touches woven throughout. On this first night of Christmas, when the snow had not yet begun to fall, it could not have been more beautiful.

"What you're forgetting is how crazy these rich people can be. I mean, I've heard of Twelve Days of Christmas, but in my house they involve canned pears and fake birds with feathers falling out—not an actual party train for the month of December." Vee walked around to the back of the table and slowly rotated one of the cake plates holding the dipped berries. Then, almost as an afterthought, she mounted a small letterpress printed card to the front of the plate. In elegant script it read: "Chocolate Dipped Strawberries" with flecks of gold across the white surface.

I gasped, "The name cards! That's what I was missing!"

"Don't worry, girl. I got it." Vee attached the other cards and then stepped back, her black and pink polka dot apron covered in frosting and sprinkles.

I sighed, scanning the table again with a critical eye. "It's flawless," I breathed. And just in time. The doorbell started ringing and that could only mean one thing: we needed to disappear.

"Quick, grab the containers."

Back in the enormous second kitchen we could truly relax—for a moment anyway. Heaven knew our work had just begun. This party would likely go on for hours, and we need to keep that gorgeous dessert table stocked the entire time.

"I know what you're thinking, and it's not in our contract to waste our whole night refilling the trays," Vee said with a little more sass than was necessary. "They have staff for that. We're only supposed to set up the table and supply the refills."

"But what if …"

"What if they put the berries where the cookies go?" Vee batted her eyes in a practiced swoon.

"Stop, Vee."

"Oh Molly, you need a life, girl."

"I *have* a life," I told her, wagging a finger. "It just so happens I love making cookies."

"Cookies you never eat," she accused. Where Genevieve Devereaux was tall elegance with generous curves and cleavage, I was slender with long legs and way less of that cleavage. A quick glance at my reflection in the oven door confirmed what I knew. The girl who looked back had bright blue eyes and blonde hair streaked with gold that could most often be found in an up-do. A swoop of bangs fell across her forehead, almost hiding a smudge of melted green chocolate. I noticed she could use a bit of concealer under those eyes—due to the lack of sleep that came with baking at wee hours of the morning—and a little lip gloss. Rubbing the chocolate off my head, I sighed and smoothed my apron. Vee was right. What I lacked in generous sleeping habits I made up for in a figure that could take a lot of cookie tastings and still remain trim.

"You know I love to dance."

"Okay, but tell me dancing works off everything you taste."

"That's the thing, I taste, … I don't do much more. You know what it's like being around sweets all the time."

"Yeah, it's tempting as hell!" Vee shook her head, patting her hips. "Now don't get me wrong, Jon loves a girl with hips, but I could use a little less jiggle in my wiggle."

"You should come dancing with me sometime. It's lots of fun."

Vee sighed, leaning back against the counter. "I'll think about it. Please just tell me we're blowing this joint. I have Christmas shopping to do."

I studied Vee's smooth brown skin as she spoke. It was a perfect cocoa butter color year round that made me slightly jealous. "You go on ahead. I won't stay much longer."

She met this statement with a frown. "Now if I come in tomorrow and you look like you've been run down by a truck, I intend to press charges."

"On the truck?"

"On my best friend who isn't taking good care of herself," Vee said pointedly. "Remember, this is a marathon, not a sprint. We're going to be doing this all month long. Pace yourself, Perfectionist Fairy."

"I'm trying," I said, going back to arranging the trays of goodies that would go in after the first wave of the night.

I heard the door close and let out a deep breath.

I'm grateful for the chance to be a Perfectionist Fairy, even if I endure ridicule.

That brought a smile to my face.

Vee was right. I needed to just go and let the hired help put out the refills. I bit my lip and looked around the room. It was a gourmet kitchen with a huge gas range, double ovens, a farm sink, and a fridge the size of my minivan. The first time I set foot inside, I had the uncontrollable urge to set up my mixer and lay out my cookie sheets. One good hour of baking in this kitchen, where there was room to stack up cooling racks and drizzle chocolate, would have been pure heaven. It was made with a baker in mind.

"You know she never uses it?"

I whirled at the sound of a male voice coming from the entrance to the hall. There stood a guy with the overly scruffy facial hair of someone who'd forgotten to shave for a week. He wore a casual pair of khakis, a shirt and tie, and a sweater vest that transformed him from the dark washed jeans of an hour earlier. I knew it was him. The biceps tipped me off. I wondered vaguely if I'd gotten all the green chocolate off my forehead and if my hastily wrapped hair was as messy as it looked just a moment ago in the oven reflection. Tucking a swath of hair behind one ear, I looked at him carefully.

"Excuse me?"

"She never uses it." He ran a hand through his dark hair scattering water droplets as he did. "She's the queen of takeout. It's a shame, don't you think, with all these gourmet appliances?"

My eyes narrowed. "I think it's a shame to talk badly about your hostess."

"Hostess," he said the word, tasting it. A smirk on his face lifted one corner of his full mouth higher than the other as he leaned his long body against the counter and surveyed me with bold blue eyes. "You're the cookie girl, right?"

I crossed my arms over the bib of my apron and lifted a brow. "The 'cookie girl'?"

"Yeah, you're the one who made all those leering Santas out there?"

I felt a tightening in my chest at the words, and my mouth dropped open. "Leering?"

"And the strawberries suffocating in their "holiday appropriate" colored chocolate?" He made air quotes.

"Suffocating?" I couldn't keep myself from repeating the offending words. He sauntered back toward the hallway with a careless air that had me ready to blow steam out of my ears. "I'll have you know ..."

"What, that you hand dipped every strawberry in your pathetic determination to please a bunch of people who are basically unpleasable? Well, don't worry. I'll digest a few handfuls of stale popcorn in your honor. 'Night, Cookie Girl."

He walked out into the hall toward the rising din of clinking glasses and clattering plates above the hum of conversation and Christmas music. His hands were in his pockets, his shoulders relaxed, as though we'd had the most pleasant conversation. I stood there gaping, offended on every imaginable level.

Stale popcorn? Leering Santas?

I whirled to examine the extra cookies, studying them from several different angles. There was no way those rosy cheeks and twinkling eyes could be considered 'leering'!

I'm grateful … ugh! Deep breath.

I'm grateful for losers who keep me humble … and furious.

I slowly loosened my fingers that had automatically balled themselves into fists, and again smoothed my hair back behind one ear in an effort to collect my volatile feelings.

Critics. There would always be at least one. I could handle critics.

I'm grateful for critics who show me what I'm made of.

Instead of busting that guy's nose and ruining his stupid preppy clothes, I would go home, change my outfit, and go dancing. The idea put a lift in my step as I went through the motions of organizing my trays one last time, casting a fleeting glance at the party room, and sneaking out the door.

* * *

"Oh no he didn't. What a loser!"

"I know, right? Can you believe he called the popcorn stale? It wasn't stale was it?"

"We popped it just before tossing it in gourmet chocolate, Molly. Why are you letting him get to you?" Vee's voice over my cell phone earpiece was just as sassy as it was in the kitchen.

"I'm not. I just …"

"He dealt a low blow to a perfectionist," Vee muttered. "Criticize a baker's baking and you've got fighting words. I'm just surprised I'm not dragging your butt out of the slammer for breaking his nose."

I grinned, pressing a hand to my forehead. "What are you talking about? I'm way more mature than that."

"Since when?"

"Look, I'm at the club. Have a fun night shopping with Jon."

"No Jon, just me and the credit card taking a few new electronics for a Christmas test drive."

"Be careful, I know how you and electronics can be," I laughed.

"Look, just because I have a designated jar of rice on my kitchen counter does *not* mean I am a liability with every device that comes into my hands. I've had this phone for—"

"Two weeks and five days," I chimed in, shutting the door of the mini and walking across the street to the dance hall.

"You're betting on how long I can keep it alive, aren't you?"

"Jon is a betting man, and I couldn't resist some easy money."

"Now, that's just not right," Vee said.

"You know we adore you and your crazy quirks."

"Hey, let's remember I'm not the only one with crazy quirks, um kay?"

Before she could go into *my* crazy quirks, I let her go and tucked away my phone. I unpinned my hair that had been twisted into a messy knot at the nape of my neck and let it flow down to my shoulders. I tussled the crown and put on lip gloss. This was Latin night at the club, and I intended to spend the next three hours forgetting about the critic at the Davenport's and reminding myself why I loved the fluid, spicy music, and the moves that came with it.

It was midnight when I took to the parking lot, fanning my face despite the chill in the air. Even though my hair was limp around my face from sweat, a smile lifted the corners of my mouth. That smile had nothing to do with the handsome guys who'd spun me around for a few numbers, but rather the way dancing made me feel. The strength and spirit of moving to the music was something I couldn't explain. I didn't need a round of drinks to lift my mood, what I needed was music and room to move. It was how I kept fit when faced with dozens of treats every day. Dancing kept me sane while dealing with the pressures of running a business and my propensity for perfectionism.

When I reached my minivan, that smile faltered.

My headlights were still on. A miserable, flickering shade of white reflecting off the night around me.

"No! No … no no no no no!"

I hurried to open the door and slide in, hoping I could preserve what little energy was left in the battery. The inside lights came on but began to flicker as I shoved the key into the ignition and chanted a revised prayer. The battery prayer was actually one I repeated quite often. This was kind of a problem I had. Maybe one of the quirks Vee would have named off if I'd let her go on earlier. Dang it! I'd been talking on the phone and had completely forgotten to turn off my lights. One turn of the key, and the indoor lights went out. The starter churned hopefully only to wind down like a neglected music box.

The battery prayer continued to go through my head as I lowered my forehead to the steering wheel.

A tap at my window did more for my heart rate than a spin around the dance floor. My head jerked up, my heart pounding, followed quickly by a lowering scowl when I recognized the face through the glass.

"Hey, you're the cookie girl, right?"

I opened the door, noticing a crowd of guys and girls heading toward the club past my car.

"What are *you* doing here?"

Sugar Cookies

Recipes from Amber Anderson owner of *From Scratch*
facebook.com/fromScratchlv

- 1 1/2 cups *unsalted* butter, room temp (3 sticks)
- 3 cups of sugar
- 1/2 Tbs vanilla extract
- 4 eggs
- 5 cups of Flour
- 2 tsp baking power
- 1 tsp salt

In a stand mixer with paddle attachment, cream together butter and sugar. Beat in eggs one at a time until well incorporated. Add vanilla extract.

In a large bowl, combine flour, baking powder, and salt. Slowly add it to wet mixture. Once combined, cover and place in the fridge for at least one hour (overnight is best).

Preheat oven to 425 degrees F. Roll onto a well-floured surface to your desired thickness. Cut with cookie cutters, or by hand, and place them on parchment lined cookie sheets one inch apart. Refrigerate again for another hour.

Once chilled through, place in oven and bake for 8-12 minutes depending on the size and thickness of your cookies.

Sugar Cookie Glaze

    4 cups confectioner's sugar
    3 Tbs milk
    3 Tbs light corn syrup
    1 Tbs almond emulsion
    1 Tbs clear vanilla extract
    food coloring paste

In a stand mixer with paddle attachment, mix confectioner's sugar, milk, and corn syrup together until combined. Add almond emulsion and vanilla extract. At this point you will want to VERY SLOWLY add milk until you receive your desired consistency.

Once complete, divide your glaze in small bowls (one for each color you will need) and add food coloring paste, mixing with a spoon.

You can now glaze your cooled cookies with a frosting spreader or fill pastry bags and use the flooding technique.

Recipes adapted from Allrecipes.com

CHAPTER TWO

Of course my humiliation would need witnesses.

He smirked, that lifting of one corner of his mouth higher than the other, and leaned against the fender of the mini.

"Hey, Greyson? Coming?"

One of the girls in the group had stopped, a hand resting on her hip. It looked as though she'd fashioned a tube top and mini skirt from a napkin, despite the rapidly dropping temps. He tossed a look over his shoulder. "Be there in a minute."

She gave me the scan, determining if I was competition. Maybe she didn't notice the way I was glaring at her boyfriend. She had nothing to worry about.

"Having some trouble?"

"Not until you walked up," I said, pulling the latch for my hood and stepping out of the car.

"Sounds like your battery."

I wanted to thank him for being a genius, but instead I lifted the hood. "Yeah, I know. Hey, your girlfriend probably wants you to go in."

"Not my girlfriend." He had both hands in his pockets. "I could give you a jump."

"Yeah, the thing is, even if you were the last person on the planet with a pair of jumper cables and a functioning battery, I would *walk* to the other end just to avoid using them."

He started laughing then, and I would never admit it to him, but the smile on his face did wonders for his limping personality. It almost made me regret the words I'd just said—almost.

"You're pissed at me."

I ignored him, walking back to the driver's side and reaching in for my phone on the front seat. Only, it was dead. Seriously? I wanted to bang my head against the window.

"I don't think those shoes are made for walking across the planet to avoid me."

I looked down at my heels and scowled. "I won't need to. Moe will help me."

"Who's that? The bartender? You'd rather ask that guy than let me give you a jump?"

"I'd rather—"

"Yes, I heard you the first time, walk to the other side of the planet, blah blah blah. How's this, I'll jump your car if you promise not to tell my mom what a jerk I was earlier.

"No thank you. And you don't have to worry. I wouldn't waste my time hunting down your mother."

"Mrs. Davenport? Won't be hard to find since you're cooking for her next party in about twenty-four hours."

I stopped my mental rampage for a moment and peered closer.

"*You're* the son of Vanessa Davenport?"

"Golden Boy, Returning Prodigal, I fit a multitude of clichés." He bowed with a low flourish at the introduction.

My head rocked back in surprise as I tried to absorb this new tidbit of information. Her *son*? Which really meant *step-son* since, if we're being honest, she could easily be his older sister. This obnoxious piece of work was the kid she was going all out for? The step-son-returned who absolutely *loved* Christmas? Thus the flurry of parties—twelve to be exact. With one for every other day in the holiday season, covering every possible celebration, complete with handmade goodies, friends, and activities. I'd honestly thought she was buying the love of a young teen. This guy was somewhere in his mid twenties, though I admit his maturity level was questionably adolescent. I shook my head in disbelief.

"You must have been quite the surprise," I said. I don't think he picked up on the derision coating my words.

"Oh, Mummy has been thoroughly disappointed in me since the moment I stepped in the house. Not only was I much older than her dear husband remembered, but I'm also entirely unpleasant to be around."

He looked so pleased with himself I felt a new wave of disgust wash over me despite the way his blue eyes kept searching my face. It made me wonder how bad my hair really looked.

"And you're making her life miserable because … she's not the old grandma with blue hair you envisioned your dad with?"

His eyes narrowed this time and he took a step nearer. "Yes, Cookie Girl. I'd hoped he had the common sense to date within his decade, or maybe one or two on either side, not a whole quarter century down the line. For crying out loud, she could be my sister!" He was almost shouting when he finished, and I tried not to smirk when he voiced my thoughts.

"Well, aren't you a little elf of happiness. Look, I'd love to participate in this little daytime talk show moment, but I've got an early morning."

"I said I'd help." He ran a hand through his hair making a mess of it.

"But then the demons might not be your friends anymore. Can't have that happening." I was already crossing the parking lot, trying not to shiver in my light dress when I heard him start his car and then rev the engine. I turned in time to see him pull a late model Mercedes in front of my van and pop his hood. I put a hand on my hip.

"What are you doing?"

"Spreading Christmas cheer," he growled as he savagely attached a pair of cables from his battery to mine.

"Ho, ho, ho," I muttered.

* * *

"Where have *you* been?"

Aunt Karen crossed the room in her fuzzy slippers and flannel pajamas. Her dark hair was the opposite of my mother's long blonde locks, but it had the same half curl that made it easy to wear natural or styled as long as they didn't mind a little unplanned chaos if the air was too humid. Tonight she wore it up on top of her head in a messy loop fastened into place with a pencil. I slumped against the door, taking a deep breath before I answered her.

"Ugh, please don't ask. I don't think I could relive this night for anyone right now. Tomorrow. Tomorrow it will be funny. That's what they say, right?"

"Bullet points then," Karen suggested, taking my face in her hands. Her eyes were the same blue as Mom's had been, too. I saw a smile in them, the same smile I always found. The one that said she didn't mind my late hours and wild stories even when her day started early the next morning.

"Annoying jerk. Dead battery. Jumped battery by annoying jerk."

"Hmm … I can't wait to hear more." She kissed my cheek, and I caught a whiff of her lotion. It smelled like an orange blossom, and immediately I felt my shoulders relax. "You know Christmas isn't just about work."

"I went dancing," I said as I crept onto the couch, exhaustion tugging me against the soft surface and squishing my cheek into a pillow.

"Good. Wait, before or after the jerk?"

"During."

"Ah …" She looked puzzled but just shrugged and walked down the hall. Her slippers scuffed into the darkness, but she paused at my last request.

"Promise me there will be waffles."

"Uncle Frank is cooking tomorrow. Waffles are his specialty, you know that."

"Then all is right with the world," I murmured before falling into black sleep.

* * *

I was in sleep's dark embrace until I smelled them. Fresh waffle batter, expertly blended and poured onto a steaming hot iron. Dozens of little pockets pressing themselves into the surface, creating the perfect receptacles for drizzled syrup—warmed, of course. Cold syrup was just a mockery of the whole process. That's what my brain was thinking before I was even fully awake.

While one section of my brain was delighting in heavenly aromas, the other was strategizing a plan to deal with Guppy. As wonderful as waking up to the scent of fresh waffles was, waking up to a dog who knows no boundaries was quite the opposite.

Guppy was a golden lab with a slobber problem. He saved it up through the night and then waited, his head on the arm of the couch, drool literally dripping down the sides of the leather into a pool on the floor. He would watch me until I opened my eyes. The moment eye contact was made, I was free game for his special brand of drool laden love.

But, I'm smarter than the average bear. For the last half hour, I could feel Guppy watching me, hear his drool drip, drip, dripping onto the floor in front of my face, and smell the warm, stinky dog breath of his pant when he opened his mouth. Without opening my eyes, I placed a hand over my face and stood slowly, feeling my way around the pool of drool in a desperate dash to the bathroom. I knew Guppy was watching, perplexed but patient for his next victim.

My cousin, Carson, was not so lucky. He was the next open-eyed human to venture into the living room, slip in the dog drool, and succumb to the excited slobbering attack of Guppy's love.

"What? Aw man! Guppy! Guuuppppyyyy!"

I giggled as I washed my hands, delighted to have side stepped the attack of the Gup. Despite the guilt of letting Carson be this morning's casualty, I couldn't help but chuckle when he threw a glare my way before going to change his shirt and wash his face. By now, having delivered his morning drool attack, Guppy would be outside trying to eat flies.

"Didja sleep well, Molly?"

"Like the black death," I said, walking into the kitchen.

"Wasn't that the plague?" Hannah looked up from the table where she was making a lake of syrup on her plate, having already filled every little pocket on her waffle.

"Yep." I sat down next to her, taking her plate and drizzling all that extra syrup over my waffle. I took a deep inhale of the sweet steam that rose up and sighed with happiness.

"Look at that, Hannah, you had two waffles worth of syrup!" Karen scolded.

"That's because she's the great syrup hog," Carson interjected, entering with a clean shirt and slightly damp hair.

"Don't call your sister a pig, it's not nice." Frank smacked the back of Carson's head as he handed him a waffle.

"I didn't call her a pig!" Carson shot Hannah a look, but Hannah only smirked. He tried flicking her ponytail in retribution. She whined and Karen interjected a scold. I sat back watching them flick and whine and scold, and smiled in contentment. This was exactly the reason I slept here every Friday night, even if it meant strategic waking to avoid Guppy. Saturday meant waffles fresh from the iron, borrowed syrup, and mayhem at the table. It was lovely.

"What's on the agenda today, Molls." Carson slid into a chair beside me and handed me one of his pieces of bacon. Carson was tall with dark hair like his mother and a round, boyish face that just needed a couple more years before it would become chiseled and handsome long enough to score a girl and then become soft and round again with the comfort of family living.

"I'm baking," I began, and Carson rolled his eyes. Saying I was baking was like saying the sun had risen in the east. I tried again. "What? Okay, I'll be more specific. I'm baking ornament cookies."

"Non-edible?"

"Made of cinnamon and some salt dough but with actual frosting decorations."

"Need help?"

"Sure, want to come cut out my cinnamons?"

Carson paused, striking a relaxed pose in his chair before announcing, "Wish I could, but I gots a date." His smile was glowing.

"A date?" I beamed at him. "And with whom, may I ask?"

"Cassidy Hill," he said, his cheeks growing scarlet when he said the name.

I rubbed his arm with pride. "Oh my gosh, you're so big!"

"Molly!"

"Sorry, okay, let me try again." I cleared my throat, wiped my silly grin, and shrugged. "Dude, that's cool. Where ya goin'?"

Carson tried not to choke on his juice. "You're a nerd."

"But a cute, endearing nerd, right?"

"Yes, cute and endearing, but definitely still a nerd. I'm taking her bowling."

I shook my head. "If I hear you're checking out the fit of her jeans—"

"Molls!" He blushed twelve shades of red.

"What? I'm just sayin'!"

"He's going to be the perfect gentleman," Karen said, sitting down next to her son and rubbing his other arm.

"He's going to be a complete dufus," Hannah said from over her teen magazine in the corner.

"Shut up!" Carson shot at her, tossing an orange segment at her magazine.

Mayhem ensued and I sat back again, beaming in pride at my family and how crazy they were. It was true. Carson would be a dufus and a gentleman, and it would be a night he would never forget.

As if on cue, after a round of scolding and whatnot, Karen turned to me.

"So, I think I should know more about your little jerk/battery jumping experience last night."

"What's this, Molly? Something about your battery?" Uncle Frank sat down with his plate full of hot waffles and asked Hannah to pass the syrup. By now there was only a quarter of the bottle left.

"Oh Frank, you can't laugh. Everyone has to be particularly solemn." I shot a look around the table knowing there was no chance at this. "I … left my lights on, and the battery was dead when I came out of the club."

"Lights?" Karen was trying not to smile.

Frank looked down as he drizzled syrup, but his brows were laughing at me anyway.

"Okay, I know … it's not the first time, but—"

"It's okay, Molly. We know you're not one hundred percent there most of the time. It's something we've come to accept." This was Carson with a consoling hand on my shoulder.

"I am running a business and getting up at 3 a.m. to bake cookies that look like Elmo and delivering and … I just forgot to check."

"Were you on your cell phone, by chance, when you got out of the car?" Karen inquired mildly.

"Can we … can we talk about my crazy night, or am I getting the third degree?"

Karen shrugged an I-told-you-so kind of shrug, but put up her hands in surrender. Frank's brows kept laughing, but he only nodded, and Carson and Hannah leaned in.

"Well, like I said, I had this huge client party. Vee and I did the dessert table with the red, gold, and green."

"Ooo, I love that one. Beautiful colors, if you ask me." Karen dipped her bacon in leftover syrup and motioned for me to continue.

"I agree," I said, grateful we'd moved past the fact that I was forgetful about car maintenance and care. I didn't mention my dead cell phone battery either. Who knew when I would hear the end of that one if it came out.

"Vee and I set everything up. I almost forgot the name cards." I shook my head to show the drama of this omission. Karen tsked. "And then, when I was in the kitchen, this total loser came in and just ripped my table apart, calling my popcorn stale and my cookies overdone. It was … the rudest …" I couldn't think of good enough adjectives that didn't involve curse words, so I left it there. "Well, who happens to show up at the club but Mr. Jerkwad himself. He called me: Cookie Girl."

"That's actually kinda cute," Karen said.

I shook my head in alarm. "What?"

"Was he hot?" Hannah put down her magazine to know this.

"Hot? No, he was an idiot! He mocked my Santas, you know, the ones with the rosy cheeks and the white beards?"

"But … what did he look like?"

I turned to her then, incredulous. "Like a jerk. What, you want details? Okay, he was, what, six foot? Dark hair. Messy. He has this half shaved beard that looks scruffy because he wants to pretend he doesn't have time to shave, but it really takes a lot of time to look half shaved. Yeah, that. It was … obnoxious, that's what it was."

"He was hot," Hannah declared. "Eyes, what color?" She was pointing at me but I couldn't tell her.

"I have no idea what that non-hot guy's eye color was. Probably brown, because the only thing I could think about was trying *not* to accidentally spray mace in his face for being a total turd." I omitted the fact that I found him incredibly handsome and actually pretty handy with car batteries. He'd had my car jumped in a matter of seconds, and he didn't look half bad in the process.

"Wow, that's pretty passionate for a complete stranger. *Teen Weekly* says some of our strongest emotions can be a mask for desire."

I tried not to make a barfing sound. "What the heck are you reading, young lady? Give me that!" I snatched her magazine and shook it at her. "These strong feelings are not masked desire unless the desire to throttle someone is what I'm masking. He was ridiculously annoying. And then he had the gall to be the only guy in the parking lot when it was sub zero temps and my battery was dead. And … wait for it …"

Uncle Frank paused with his fork in midair. The corners of his mustache were twitching.

"He's the reprobate stepson of my biggest client. The Twelve Days of Christmas kid. Only he's not a kid. He's an adult who has no self respect, and I honestly think he might hate Christmas."

"Oh!" Karen was sufficiently impressed by this revelation.

I'd lost Carson after the first sentence, and Hannah was only listening because she thought he was hot and now she knew he was loaded too.

"Did you get his number?" she asked, leaning forward so that the end of her braid dipped into her syrupy plate.

"No, I did not get his number, syrup girl," I said. "And with that fine news, I must bid you all adieu while I go make dozens of beautiful cookies for the Davenports." Turning to Carson, I tapped my cell phone. "I want to hear all the deets after tonight, young man, including the number of times you held the door for this cute Hill girl."

"Yes, ma'am," he said, coloring again but still smiling in that way that told me he was excited to have something to tell. Ah, young love.

"Let me come out and check on your battery," Uncle Frank volunteered.

"No, no," I insisted. "I'll come in if it doesn't start right up. This isn't my first rodeo," I told him.

He smiled then, standing to hug me. "See you next week?"

"Or maybe sooner if things get too crazy dealing with this guy all month."

"You know you're always welcome," Karen called, blowing me a kiss.

"Thanks," I said, walking to the door. Guppy looked up at me from his blanket, too tired, or lazy at this point, to care that he hadn't given me his traditional slobbery greeting. "Next time, Gup," I said, and he tipped his muzzle in agreement before I shut the door.

* * *

The entire van smelled like cinnamon, and I was in a super Christmasy mood as Vee and I drove to the Davenport's the next day. The van was packed to the ceiling with pink bakers' boxes filled with ornament cookies.

"I think it's cool that they're using cookies for both their trees."

"Yeah, I cannot believe how wonderful this is. I mean, the salt doughs were pretty labor intensive," I sighed, thinking of the hours I'd spent putting gold details on the cookies before carefully packing them into the van, "but they turned out fantastic. I posted a bunch of pics on the website, and I've already received a lot of interest."

"Just in time for you to open a shop of your own."

I grinned, leaning my head against the head rest, thinking about the small but perfect space on Fifth and

Main where I envisioned my shop coming to life. There would be a couple huge ovens, a glass case for all the beautiful cookies we sold, and a consult room for special events. "This season is going to put us over the top. I can't wait to get my hands on that place."

"The Cookie Jar will be a hit all over town. Just watch." Vee's smile and energy were infectious. I beamed at her as we pulled into the back driveway at the Davenport's rambling estate house.

Clouds were gathering overhead that spoke of snow and hinted at Christmas, while turning each breath to ice crystals that smoked up the air. It made me grateful for the driveway that led almost directly to the back door of the kitchen. It would make unloading especially easy in the stormy days ahead.

"Don't look now, but I think that hot cocoa guy is back. You know, the one with the nice jeans the other night?" Vee made an appreciative sound at the backside turned toward us. But I was not looking in appreciation; I was looking in recognition of that backside. Not the backside. Please! I was looking at the messy hair and the unshaved stubble along his jaw. Ugh! That backside belonged to none other than the misery making stepson I'd become too well acquainted with in the club parking lot. When I told Vee, she turned to stare over her shoulder. "Doesn't look like a rich guy. Those shoulders and biceps are way too built for someone who spends their life holding out their hand for the next payout."

"Maybe he does pushups between every swipe of the family credit card, but believe me when I tell you his jeans and biceps don't make up for his attitude. He is toilet water leaked onto a public bathroom floor. Yes! That disgusting."

"Wow, someone got to you girl." Vee was grinning in that way she did when she thought she knew something I didn't.

"Just … help me." She did, opening the door and holding it while I balanced baker's boxes into the kitchen.

"Molly! I'm so glad you're here. We just got the trees set up. Come see!" Mrs. Davenport led the way into the grand foyer with its vaulted ceiling and gorgeous mosaic medallion in the center of the floor. Placed in the middle was a lean and tall pine that challenged the chandelier for supremacy. It came very close to touching the light, but stopped just shy.

"Oh, it's amazing," I whispered, inhaling the fabulous scent of freshly cut pine.

"I know, isn't it? James helped us choose them, and he has a magnificent eye—don't you, honey?"

Mr. James Davenport walked in, looking refreshed and tan like he'd just been out on the golf course. I could im-

COOKIE GIRL CHRISTMAS · 39

mediately see the resemblance between him and his smart-mouthed son. The elder had the same strong jaw line and wavy dark hair, though his was touched with a distinguished shade of gray here and there. And he had the same broad shoulders—though, at a glance, the younger had the better biceps and more ruggedly built physique. I hated to think Vee was right about that.

"It looks great, honey. Now where are these ornaments you wanted me to hang?"

"In the kitchen. We'll have them all laid out in five minutes and you can start whenever you're ready," I said, then hurried back to the kitchen where Vee was—flirting with the rich boy.

"Hey there, Cookie Girl. I see your battery is back in working order."

"I'm here," I said.

Vee raised a nicely manicured brow in my direction, a gesture that said she noticed I'd left something out of the report she'd wrangled from me on the drive over. Like the whole part about running into this guy. But I could see I was right. He was definitely built better than Mr. Davenport, with an underlying muscular structure that drew my eyes back to him several times more than it should have.

"We kind of got off on the wrong foot," he said to Vee. His voice was low and he leaned in, trying to turn on the charm. Vee giggled and I fought the urge to roll my eyes. It still amazed me what a little bit of chin scruff and intense blue eyes could do to a girl. I shot her a look but she wasn't paying attention.

Thank goodness that working an event takes my total concentration. I let their conversation slide into the background while I worked, placing the cookies in perfect lines on the trays, grateful we'd decided to insert the ornament hangars the night before. One of the lace tray covers was crooked, and I worked to get it just right, stepping back several times to check the angle.

To be honest, being a designer is a borderline celebration of obsessive compulsive disorder. Clients want an eye for detail and a knack for figuring out the perfect touch to make a simple dessert beautifully elegant. A good event planner does a delicate tango between letting details slide for their own sanity, and going above and beyond for the client.

Vee calls it the Cookie Zone, when everything goes quiet and I hone in on the project at hand. That's where I was now, in the Cookie Zone, as I laid out the trays and stood back to examine the overall balance. Meticulously decorated cookies stars, candy canes, and Santas awaited their moment to shine. The snowmen were my favorite, with their striped scarves and carrot noses. They reminded of me of my mother and those fuzzy memories I held on to with both hands: building snowmen and dreaming of them coming to life while I slept, skating at the rink until our noses were too cold to properly sniffle anymore, and then finding refuge in a steaming cup of cocoa. Baking with her in our kitchen stood out most of all, times when she would gently put her hands over mine, helping me roll out dough and press the cookie cutters into the soft surface. For me, it was magic turning a lump of dough into smooth shapes that could come to life with tubes of colored frosting.

Of course, I was there for the pinches of sweet dough, the finger-fuls of frosting, and the tossers. Those were the ones that baked up too puffy or the colors smeared when we frosted them. Those were mine.

After practicing the craft myself, I knew well that Mom made many of those mistakes just for me. The thought filled my chest with a kind of aching I'd learned to manage, a pain that used to sear through me on a daily basis and now only managed to ease in when I let down my guard. Though the pain had dulled in recent years, there would never be a time when I didn't think of Christmas and miss my mom. Oh, how she loved Christmas. With the first carol of the season, her eyes would well with tears. I remember the embarrassment that haunted me as a teenager at seeing my mom wipe her eyes. I can still recall my share of rolled eyes and exasperated sighs at her emotion. It shocked me how those memories hurt my heart. What I wouldn't give now to see her beautiful blue eyes filling with tears when the first "Silent Night" came over the air waves. Once that possibility was gone, it was all the more cherished. It was part of what made her amazing.

Even now, with my hands full of cookies, an apron tied around my hips, and my hair flipped into a ponytail, I felt a longing for her that never seemed to ebb. I closed my eyes for a moment, with the sounds of Christmas all around me, and imagined what she would do if she were here, if that dreaded disease hadn't taken her from a healthy, laughing woman to a shell: frail, tired, ready— ready to be done with Christmases. The thought made me catch my breath and my eyes flew open.

"You okay, Cookie Girl?"

He was watching me. When I opened my eyes they met his, and for one second there was nothing to shelter me from his searching gaze. He had blue eyes, the color of a dark stormy sky with crinkling around the edges that said at one time he had laughed a lot. I'd have to remember to tell Hannah. But it was the plain inquiry in them that caught me off guard. They narrowed when they caught a glimpse of my insides, the parts I worked hard to protect from sight. Forcing my eyes to the floor, I ducked down pretending like I'd dropped a cookie.

I'm grateful for nosy losers who don't mind their own business.

"Don't you have some starving children to mock or some Christmas presents to steal?" I asked as I straightened again with my sacrificial cookie in hand. It was a candy cane with red sugar pressed in between stripes of white icing.

"I'm waiting for Christmas Eve when I can saddle up my fake-antlered dog and sneak down all the chimneys in Whooville. It's so much more fun than a preemptive strike." He was still looking at me. Too closely. It did something terrible to my insides, something that made me catch my breath. It was annoying.

"Well, don't let me keep you from whatever dastardly deeds you've planned for today."

"To be honest," he stepped closer, his hands in his pockets, "I'm stuck here playing Christmas with my stepmommy and her little henchmen."

"You mean her kids?"

"You call them your thing, I call them mine."

"They're your half siblings, right?"

"If I still claimed lineage."

"Your $200 loafers say you do," I said, going back to the trays.

There was a smirk. "You think I spend my Daddy's money?"

I turned on him with an angelic smile, desperately grateful for the turn in our conversation, and that he wasn't the kind of jerk who kept pushing when I didn't want to talk about things.

"Isn't that what all you trust fund brats do?" I sauntered past him with a tray on each arm, catching a whiff of something that smelled amazing. Could it be his cologne? If it was, I wanted to stick my nose to his neck and take a deep breath. Resisting such a Guppy-like urge, I pointed myself to the family room, where another enormous Christmas tree was displayed, and made a mental note to spend less time with Guppy. Vee was there, arranging a spray of evergreens and holly studded with red berries along a table. I added the trays and stood back with a satisfied smile.

"Ah, it's perfect," Mrs. Davenport said, clicking into the room on three inch heels and a dress that was more clubbing than Christmas tree decorating attire. Two little girls tripped in after her, their eyes growing in size every time they touched a different detail. It was their reaction alone that would have me walking on air for days.

"Mommy! It's Christmas! It's really Christmas!"

"Can we touch? I know you told us not to touch, but …"

The older one shushed the younger one and clasped her hands together anxiously as they awaited their mother's reply. She turned to look at them with glowing eyes. "This party is for you too, girls! We're decorating the tree with these amazing cookies!"

"*We* can do it?" The girls looked at each other in shock, and I knew from that look that the trees in their past were to be seen not touched. It made me adore my mother all the more for letting me basically wreak havoc on our tree from year to year. She was more a making memories mom than a magazine design-page-diva.

"Of course! This tree is for all the children. Greyson!"

I tried to hide a smile at the thought of Greyson being involved with the children's tree. The number of years that separated the little girls at my feet and the man in the kitchen could not have been less than fifteen.

Greyson appeared at the doorway, his smirk back in place, a general glower in his eyes.

"You called?" There was a dryness to his tone that made Vee's grin broaden. She loved a good smart aleck.

"It's time!" Mrs. Davenport clapped her hands together in what could only be blonde delight, and Greyson looked like he was resisting the urge to say something heinous. I smothered a smile and found his eyes on me again. That was our sign to melt into the background.

We brought in another couple trays. The tree in this room wasn't anything close to the towering specimen in the entry hall, but I was glad I'd overestimated during the baking and decorating phase. While the "kids" decorated with squeals of delight and lots of half panicked direction from their mother—who really must have been a perfectionist after all—Vee and I decorated some simple cookies and heated a pot of hot cocoa for the family to enjoy after the festivities.

"I think he likes you," Vee said with that mischievous twinkle in her eyes. I ignored that tingling in my chest at the idea while setting out the cookies and mugs. Instead, I flashed her a look that said she was crazy.

"You are all sugared up. How did your shopping trip for the man go?"

She held up a hand to tell me she wasn't done with her train of thought. "And, he's hot."

Why did people keep saying that? "Is this about the beard thing on his face?"

"You mean the sexy scruff he has going on? Um … yeah, that's a nice feature, but that's not the only one, and you know it."

"We have cleanup to do."

Vee shook her head and dusted off her apron with her long caramel colored fingers. "You can change the subject all you want, but I'm calling it right now. You know I just want to see you find a nice guy who makes you happy."

"I *am* happy, without the guy to complicate matters," I told her, gathering the bags of frosting and extra trays, and heading out to the van.

"Complications can be fun."

"No, complications are complicated. They don't make life interesting, they make life stressful and, more often than not, painful. I'm okay with my uncomplicated life."

She blew out a breath and helped me with my load before going back in to wipe down the counters to leave everything spotless. Inside the van she looked at me, "When do we start the marshmallows?"

"Tomorrow," I waved away her question, "with the homemade candy canes."

* * *

With frost buffering the edges of the metal benches and blanketing the table, the idea of making a hot cocoa bar following an afternoon of ice skating that had sounded delightful only twenty-four hours earlier suddenly seemed less appealing. There would be fresh gingerbread men for dunking, homemade marshmallows in the shape of stars for melting, and hand pulled candy canes for swirling a hint of mint into their cup. It all sounded very Christmas romantic until I pulled into the parking lot at the outdoor rink and stared at the thermometer on my minivan.

The temperature hadn't risen much from the day before when the world went white with a winter storm. I'd worked just fine while indoors, the ovens keeping me warm while I boiled sugar and cut marshmallows. Today was still freezing even though the snow had stopped falling for a few hours. The walkways were treacherous, and our small outdoor burner would barely clear the snow pile outside the rink. My fingers were turning numb just thinking about what lay ahead.

This event would be more relaxed for us since the rink as the main entertainment. Yet there was plenty to do in preparation. Vee had a decorating epiphany the night before that included twinkle lights strung around a tented covering. The tent was in case of snow, which was highly likely on a gray day like this one, and the twinkle lights added a dash of festive spirit. I was all about festive spirit. It was the frigid cold and my fingers that didn't get along.

A knock on my window made me jump. Vee, I'd expected. What I hadn't bargained for was the guy standing next to her.

Frank's Saturday Waffles

Recipe from Christene Houston

    2 c. flour

    2 Tbsp. sugar

    4 tsp. baking powder

    ¾ tsp. salt

    2 eggs

    1 ½ c. milk

    ¼ c. melted butter

    1 tsp. vanilla extract

Mix all dry ingredients in a large bowl.

In a separate bowl, beat eggs then add milk, butter and vanilla.

Add wet ingredients to dry ingredients and beat until well blended.

Pour portions into a preheated waffle iron, and cook until golden and slightly crispy.

CHAPTER THREE

Greyson Davenport was hunched up behind Vee, his shoulders drawn round under the oppressive cold, his nose pink, and his eyes sparkling bluer above the blue muffler he wore.

After a moment of indecision, where I considered ignoring them until he disappeared, I rolled the window down and gasped at the rush of cold.

"We're going to turn into snowmen," Vee chattered. No matter how much she claimed to have extra padding for warmth, that girl was always cold. Her fingers were perennial ice picks, and her toes—let's just say nobody wanted to share the couch blanket with that girl after an outing in the snow. Ice cold toes were always her gift, usually pressed against warm legs or, if she was extra sneaky, behind a back.

"Another one of my precious Mummy's ideas." Greyson groaned looking toward the rink.

"Why did you bring him?" I lowered my voice a little, not terribly worried I'd hurt his feelings.

"Don't we need help with the tent?" Vee looked like I'd missed the obvious.

"Um, where is Jon? Isn't he the guy you're hoping to marry?"

"Yes, he is," I lost her for a moment in the silly love-bird haze that often came over her when Jon was mentioned, "but he's working. He did help me check the lights last night."

"You mean last night while I was cutting out a thousand star shaped marshmallows all by myself?"

I got out of the car and cast one last longing look at the seat warmer button before slamming the door.

"You're not being very Christmasy, Miss Hayes." Vee looked offended.

"I think my Christmas is frozen."

"Won't be the only thing in a couple minutes," Greyson chimed in. He looked a little too cheerful about that so I chose to ignore him.

"Look, let's just get the tent up before those clouds dump on us, and then we'll set up the stove and the table."

Vee walked with me to the back of the minivan and began unloading supplies while Greyson looked on.

"Are you sure he knows that he's supposed to be helping?" I hissed to Vee as we manhandled the pipes and tarp for the tent onto the sidewalk, slipping twice.

"I think he knows he should, but maybe he doesn't know how."

I noticed him gazing thoughtfully at the rink, with only his eyes visible above his muffler. He looked like he was in another time and place. I had the faintest impression that something was off with him. From the few times I'd been in his presence, a smart mouth usually came along with the package. Today he was much more reserved.

"Um … could use a hand here," I shot at him as we passed again with the heavy gas burner and propane tank.

"Sure, be there in a sec …" He didn't move.

I looked at Vee but she could only shrug and mouth the word, "Sorry!"

We set up as he leaned against the fence surrounding the skating rink and watched the skaters. With all the heavy lifting, I wasn't cold anymore, but perhaps there was more heat than normal coming from my rising irritation at the guy who'd come along to lend a hand. Talk about chivalry being dead. I had to think of happy things to stop myself from forming a hard packed snowball and aiming for the back of his annoying head.

I'm grateful for loser rich kids who help me get warm by not helping.

"You need to stop glowering at the boss's son," Vee whispered when we hefted the heavy pot out of the back of the van, each taking a handle with mittened hands and waddling our way to the burner.

"I'm trying," I said. We strung the lights around the white tent edges next and plugged them in the electrical outlet near the rink. By now Greyson had skates on and was zipping around the rink with his hands behind his back.

"It's not working."

With him safely out of earshot I spun on Vee. "What the heck, Vee? Since when do you bring strays?"

"I went by the house because I left my new headphones when we were cleaning up after the cookie ornaments. That cookie tree looks pretty dang good, by the way."

"Of course it does," I muttered, arranging the trays of shaped marshmallows while she placed the candy canes in hot drink cups.

"Well, I saw him just sulking around and asked what he was doing."

"You don't *have* to say everything that comes into your head; you know that, right?"

"And what fun would that be?" she asked, narrowing her eyes at me, tossing her fluffy brown curls and putting a hand on one softly rounded hip. "He looked lonely and I don't do lonely."

"He's lonely because he has the personality of a cactus. People tend to prefer acupuncture from a Japanese medical professional."

"Not Japanese, Chinese."

"The point," I said, scowling so she would know I was serious, "is that he is not welcome here. Not with us. This is a business, and while I understand that his mommy is paying our salary during this whole ... thing ... we're still *working*—not flirting, not helping cactuses."

"Cacti."

"Whatever."

"Okay, sorry. I really thought he wanted to help."

I paused and watched him spin in ever widening circles, his hands extended, his face sad. I closed my eyes to block out the sight before turning to her. "You're forgiven. Just don't let it happen again."

"You have to admit my tent idea was genius."

She was right. The twinkle lights were romantic and tempting in the gray light of the day. It drew the attention of passersby on their way to the rink. I was glad we'd put our Cookie Jar sign out. Maybe a shop of my own next year wasn't a complete shot in the dark.

Just then, Mrs. Davenport pulled up in a huge, shiny SUV but didn't get out. I watched her for a moment, her shades in place on a dark day and wondered if she was watching her surprise step son move around the rink.

"Be right back." I walked through the snow to her car, waving as I approached. I saw her swipe at her cheeks and roll down her window.

"Hi, Vanessa. You're going to love the hot cocoa bar we've arranged."

"It looks lovely, Molly. It really does." A long silent pause, a sniff and then, "I just don't think it's going to work."

I hugged myself to keep from shivering. "Want to talk about it?"

She adjusted her sunglasses and sniffled before her lip began to tremble and another flood of tears appeared on her cheeks.

"It's Greyson. He's completely ruining everything!"

I tried not to tell her I agreed with her assessment. Instead I thought of something nice to say like, "Is there anything I can do?"

"He said he loved Christmas," she swiped at her tears angrily and shook her head, "but if by love he meant he loved making fun of my trees and insulting my guests, then he definitely loves Christmas. He disappears at a moment's notice. I try to play what is supposed to be his favorite Christmas song and he storms out of the room. I even found some old ornaments he and his sister made, and he almost threw them across the room. When I asked him to come today, he said he would rather—well, I'm not going to repeat his statement because it was very inappropriate. But now look at him!"

She wiped a tear from her cheek and sucked in her bottom lip. "I admit I thought I could make him like me by doing all this fun and festive stuff. But he hates me, and I don't think it will ever change, no matter how many cookies I throw at him."

We both looked at him skating around the rink, and I wiped a snowflake from my cheek. "Sounds like he's a complete Scrooge."

"And I'm Tiny Tim, all adorable and cheerful in the midst of adversity," Mrs. Davenport sniffled.

A bubble of laughter threatened to escape from the comparison, but I coughed instead and then bit my lip before turning back to the window.

"I'm sorry this isn't turning out how you'd like. Christmas is supposed to be the time of year when you get away from the everyday troubles."

She nodded thoughtfully, putting her sunglasses atop her head and wiping at her eyes with manicured fingers. "Yes, it is. That's what I love about Christmas. Sometimes it's just nice to be happy and make dreams come true. It's fun to love Christmas."

"Yeah, my mom was a huge fan of this time of year."

"It shows in your work, Molly. She must have been amazing."

Mrs. Davenport looked at me with a sympathetic smile, and I just shrugged. "She was. Absolutely."

There was another small pause where she looked down at the steering wheel while my toes began to freeze in my boots.

I'm grateful for boots that keep my toes warm when I'm not standing in a pile of snow.

When she looked up she was smiling so wide I could see all her freshly whitened teeth gleaming at me. "You know what? I think you're absolutely right. Christmas is about getting away! Of course it is! That's where I've gone wrong. Maybe being in the house where his parents broke up is bringing out painful memories. What he needs is a getaway, and I know just the place."

I stared at her, trying to recall saying something that would have inspired this sudden burst of enthusiasm.

"Sure ... something different ... like a work camp?"

"Ha ha, you're so funny, Molly." She tapped my hand with her leather gloved ones. "Not a work camp, something much better."

"Hmm ... that would work for me," I murmured, catching another glimpse of him flashing by.

"When we were first married, we went to this incredibly romantic little inn up in the mountains not far from here. Last time we checked, it was under poor management and we haven't been back in years. But I've heard the old owners have resumed care and they were fabulous. It was summertime when we went last, but I can only imagine how it would look frosted in snow and decked out in holiday colors. We could invite a few other families to join us and carry on this whole plan up there. It's only about an hour away, they have a good kitchen—we could bring everything with us."

"Oh?"

My mind was going a hundred miles a minute with all the logistics of moving my operation so many miles up a steep mountainside. The packing alone was intimidating.

"Are you sure we can get there with this weather?"

"I'll make all the arrangements. Bring Vee, all your supplies ... in fact, I'll lend you one of our 4-wheel drive vehicles just to be safe. I don't think the mini will make it up there."

"Mm-hmm." I was trying to think of a way to back up the party train and keep it in the city. I was grateful for the city, a place where I didn't have to worry about being snowed in for more than a few hours. What if I forgot

COOKIE GIRL CHRISTMAS · 59

something? There were ingredients to gather, table cloths, props—the list was endless, and already I was falling behind just thinking about it.

"This is such a splendid idea, Molly. I can't thank you enough. You always know what to do!"

"Me? I am resourceful like that." My voice sounded far away.

"What's going on over here? I think the cocoa is ready to ladle out." Vee wrapped an arm around my waist, her warmth sinking into my rapidly freezing bones.

"We're moving the whole Operation Twelve Days of Christmas to the mountains," I told her, looking into her face. She was quick to note the panic in my face that overrode the false cheer in my voice. She hugged me tighter and turned to Mrs. Davenport.

"Oh, is that even possible? Think of all we'll have to bring. The sprinkles, the gingerbread house pans, the crystal cake stands … I don't know, Molly. I don't want to rain on anyone's parade, but I'm worried. It could be pretty labor intensive."

"I hadn't considered the strain it would put on you both." Mrs. Davenport's forehead drew into the perfect little scowl, but only for a moment. "I would definitely cover your travel and lodging, but perhaps if I doubled our original payment it would make up for the extra effort?"

I was still looking at Vee, and my eyes must have been huge because her smile grew exceptionally bright. "It sounds like a deal, Mrs. Davenport."

"Lovely!" Her face looked determined. "I'll notify our staff immediately. It will mean no skating today, but I insist the cocoa be put to good use. There are a lot of cold skaters on the ice this afternoon. Let's share it with them. Just be sure they know it's from the Davenports."

"Will do." Vee was still being spokesperson, because the planner in my brain had been initiated and was running full throttle.

"Thank you, Molly, Vee. We're going to get that kid to love Christmas—and me—after all."

With that, she pulled her SUV into the gently falling snow and disappeared in a cloud of steam.

* * *

Snow fell gently during the ride up the mountain. It had taken four days of planning and packing, in between the Nutcracker and cookie exchange parties, to get to this point. Snowflake Falls Inn was just as romantic as Vanessa had described. Located at the end of a well plowed road set deep in the mountains, it stood in a cozy nook made by the rocks themselves. Tucked in amongst the pines and aspens, the inn was three stories tall. A wide front porch yawned its way across the building, tempting the travel worn to put their feet up in a rocking chair or two. Something about the snow frosting the roof tops, and the rustic welcome sign over the door, made one feel like it was just the place to get away—that is, until stepping foot in the ice strewn parking lot.

"I'm grateful for spotty parking lot maintenance that helps me practice my ice skating skills." It was a grumble, as I tested out my next step with a box full of sprinkles in one hand and the other hand tugging along a suitcase on wheels.

"You know you're saying that out loud, right?" Vee whooped as she almost slipped and took a case full of fondant with her.

"I'm grateful for an exceptionally graceful business partner."

"Well, I would be grateful for some salt and one of those golf carts," Vee giggled, trying to maintain her balance.

"I'm grateful for golf carts." I tried not to laugh at the stance Vee took after her next wobble over ice.

"I know it helps you when you're stressed to think of the things you're grateful for, but do you really think being thankful for golf carts is going to make one appear?"

I shimmied through another ice patch and gasped as my suitcase flopped over on its face.

"Sometimes just being thankful is enough," I said. I made sure my feet were planted on pavement before wrenching my suitcase back into a standing position.

"Maybe we should call ahead for reinforcements," Vee whimpered, frozen in one position after a particularly dreadful moment where fondant almost went flying.

"I can't believe this! I mean, someone could break a hip! It's a liability."

"Are you two old ladies, now?"

Ugh. How did I know that voice so well already? Greyson Davenport was standing at the parking lot gate with both hands in the pockets of his corduroy jacket. There was an undeniable smirk of enjoyment on his face. I wondered how long he'd been standing there watching us slip around.

"If you're here for Ice Capades, you'll need to buy a ticket."

"How much? 'Cause this is priceless."

I was ready to throw sprinkles at his head, but Vee took a different approach, "Get in here and rescue us, cowboy."

And he did. Just like that. Vee first, of course. He bent down and picked up a pail of salt and started spreading it out onto the pavement around him as he made his way to her. She looked up at him with those big brown eyes and a ready smile. "My hero!"

Extending his arm, he helped her to the sidewalk leading up to the inn, which I assumed was free of ice. She didn't stop to be sure I was indeed rescued.

I'm grateful for treacherous friends who save themselves while leaving me to die or be rescued by him.

Greyson turned back to me, the pail still in his hands. "Need a hand out there?"

"That, or test out our broken hip theory." I was trying not to grit my teeth in frustration.

"Oh, that's right. You two eighty-year-old ladies were in fear for your hips."

He walked back the same way he'd come—only in my direction this time—making a wide circle around me as he scattered salt and then stopped right in front of me.

"I could take your suitcase."

"I'm fine."

"Sprinkles by the case?"

"I am a cookie decorator."

"Cookie *Girl*."

"Actually, my shop is named *The Cookie Jar*."

"Yeah, I know." He grinned down at me like he knew something I didn't.

"Well, thanks for the salt."

"Yep."

I waited for him to go so I could, too, but he didn't move. He was looking over my shoulder toward the once shiny SUV I'd driven up in.

"Um … I'm going to the inn before my fingers freeze off."

"Sure. Good idea. Just … are you leaving your lights on in hopes of another rescue or just for giggles and grins?"

White Hot Chocolate

Recipe from Jamie Burt

2 cups whipping cream

6 cups milk

1 teaspoon vanilla

1 (12 oz) package white chocolate chips

Note: this recipe tastes the best with a premium white chocolate chip, not vanilla flavored chips.

Stir together the whipping cream, milk, vanilla, and white chocolate chips in a slow cooker.

Cover and cook on low for 2 to 2 1/2 hours, stirring occasionally, until mixture is hot and chips are melted.

Stir again before serving.

Chapter Four

I turned to look. Grr. He was totally right. Vee was going to get a kick out of this.

"Just for giggles," I murmured.

I'm grateful for good looking, obnoxious men who save me from total embarrassment … kind of.

After turning my lights off, we navigated the frozen walk. A couple stood on the porch shielded from the breeze that picked its way beneath my scarf and weaseled in the gaps in my coat. The man towered in height and had more than a passing resemblance to a mountain man —complete with a beard that could make him an easy stand in for Santa Clause. The woman beside him was a lesson in contrasts, tall and elegant next to his wild scruffiness. Her orangey red curls were tastefully streaked with white and piled atop her head. She wore a ruffled apron that immediately inspired a pang of apron envy in my chest.

She grinned as we reached the steps. "Welcome to Snowflake Falls Inn, and Merry Christmas!"

"Thank you. Merry Christmas." It felt good to step onto the solid wood of the porch step after all that sliding.

"You must be the baker," she said, eying my case of sprinkles.

"Guilty," I said, extending a hand while casting a sidelong glance at the mountain of a human standing beside her. "Molly Hayes from The Cookie Jar."

"I'm Mama Lucille, and this is Big Ben. Now don't get all politically correct and anxious. He's a big man and he likes being called Big Ben. Our daughter, Lennox, is one of those girls who gets plenty irritated when people get all uppity about things. No need to be uppity."

I wanted to tell her she was in for quite a bit of uppity with this group, but I decided to smile instead and say, "You won't get no sass from me."

"That'll be a first," Greyson grumbled behind me.

"What's that young man?"

Lucille's amber brows arched. She may have had an apron around her hips, but she was all business. I liked her immediately.

"This one, she's sassy." Greyson must not have read that arch the way I did.

But instead of telling him to mind his manners, her eyes flicked between the two of us with a knowing look, a look that I wanted to wipe from her face.

"We're not together," I said, talking too quickly. "He's a Davenport."

"Mm-hmm," she hummed. "The shoes tipped me off."

"I've got some wood to be choppin' if you're done with me," Ben said. His voice was deep and gravelly and he looked very much like a child being made to wear a tie for church.

She gave him a wink. "You go on then." I don't think I imagined the pink that tinged his cheeks right above the white of his beard. He ducked his head and brushed his lips against her cheek before lumbering down the porch.

Greyson waited next to me with his bucket of salt, watching Lucille. I couldn't tell what he thought of her with his brows pulled down low. I shifted the box in my hands. "Could you show me to the kitchen?"

"'Course. Your room is top floor, Davenport."

"Greyson," he said. "And I can help if there's anything else you need." The words shocked me. Like he'd just admitted to where he hid the body. Was this the same guy who had 'helped' at the skating rink? What was next, the zombie apocalypse? I walked ahead of them into the inn.

Mama Lucille, however, did not think his offer so strange. She took his arm, weaving her own through it.

"You've done good, Greyson," she said. "Let it be known that chivalry is not completely dead. Just wounded."

"Maybe gushing blood," Greyson agreed.

"Nothing a few good stitches won't fix up right," she continued, following me into the inn. "You know, it's a regular Christmas miracle the way your mama called and booked this place up."

"Step-mom." I could hear the wince in Greyson's voice.

"We sold to our son-in-law a few years back … boy was that a mistake." She blew out a long breath and rolled her shoulders. "It's taken us all this time to recoup one six month stretch under his management. Long-time guests refused to return. Our inn has been at half capacity for quite some time. Your visit this Christmas has filled us right back to the top with only one room left."

"That's a shame about your son-in-law," I said.

Lucille looked over at me, her brow troubled. "Yeah. Lennox thinks so, too. She got caught in the middle, poor thing. I just hope she can recover now that she's on her own again." She led us down a hall lined with landscapes painted in oil.

"This is her." Lucille stopped before a family portrait that hung amidst the wall decor. She pointed out a smiling redhead with braces and frizzy hair. She nudged Greyson. "She always says she's going to come back and burn this picture. I'm hoping it will get her here, and then we can do the rest."

I grinned. "I'm sure it's not the family part. It's more the braces and hair."

"She's a librarian in her little town. Her beagle, Hades, keeps her active."

"She named her dog after the underworld?"

"She was living in it for a while there." Lucille shrugged. "I guess it just made sense at the time."

Walking on, I could see the kitchen open up and felt a familiar thrill at the sight. "This is me. Nice to meet you, Lucille."

"I'll be back 'round when I've made sure our guests are comfy," Lucille said, touching my shoulder. "You holler if you're needing anything."

"I will," I said, casting Greyson a wary glance. Something was different about him. Maybe Vanessa was right. Maybe he needed to get away from the house and the city. Maybe the real Greyson was showing himself after all.

"I like hot cocoa with gingerbread," he tossed over his shoulder as they walked away. "Have some sent up to my room—wouldja, Cookie Girl?"

Then again, maybe not.

* * *

We were walking down the pathway to our cabin when I told Vee about my headlights.

"The lights? No way. That's twice in just over a week. Girl, you're on a roll."

"Can we not talk about the lights? You were there too, ya know. It just so happens you were already inside the inn when he noticed."

"He sure gets under your skin, doesn't he?"

"Like a chigger." I itched my forearm just thinking about it, "Let's talk about something else."

"The kitchen is fabulous."

"I know," I sighed. "I wish I had money to put something like that into the bakery."

"It's true, it would be awesome, but there's nothing wrong with baby steps," Vee said.

I'm grateful for baby steps.

I stamped my feet on the snow covered walkway. Up ahead, the cabin came into view. It was a sweet set-up. Inn guests were put up in the luxuriously decorated rooms in the main house, while the rest of us were given cabins a short distance out the back door and tucked in among the trees and snow. I simply adored the idea. We stashed almost all of our supplies in the kitchen at the inn, and brought the rest with us down the little path that led to our home in the woods. It was quaint, romantic perfection at its best, and the effect was felt immediately.

We peeked inside, adoring the cozy fireplace, the overstuffed chairs, the soft throw. Even the bathroom was darling with it's clawfoot tub and gilded mirror. The huge bed in the bedroom was covered in a down comforter so fluffy I had to flop onto it at once.

"This place is so dreamy. If I invite Jon up here are you going to kill me?" Vee asked while I relished the softness of the down beneath me.

"Yes. With that plunger in the bathroom."

"Ew. I never noticed your bathroom fixation before. But it's Christmas! I can hardly believe I'm up here with icicles and snowflakes and kisses under the mistletoe to seal everlasting love, and he's not."

Vee sank down beside me and I sat up catching sight of her face. She looked adrift. She and Jon were hardly ever separated, and this was a true test of her fortitude. I tried not to be Grinchy even though thinking about true love felt hollow to me.

"We'll be too busy to even notice," I assured her, taking her hand to comfort her and hopefully banish the thought of an attack by plunger. "You'll be home by Christmas morning, and who would not want to have you as their real live Christmas present?"

Vee shrugged unconvinced but said, "Fine, but I'm going to need a few days off during this whole Twelve Days of Christmas. Somewhere around the Five Golden Rings and Ten Drummers Drumming."

"Okay, let's say you go back to the city on the movie night and the day we do the sleigh rides?"

She thought for a moment, counting the days in her head until she could smooch on her sweetheart again. "That's fair. You can make me a list of anything we missed when we packed up, and I'll bring them back."

"Deal." I grinned at her, glad to see her smiling again as she put the dates into her phone. Vee was a fantastic partner, and I wanted her to be happy.

After looking around, I unpacked, certain my mind would quit spinning if I got organized. When it was still firing like a Chinese firecracker—my clothes safely entombed in the rustic dresser, my toothbrush happily waiting by the sink, and my jingle bell bracelet perched with anticipation on the dresser top—I decided a quick walk through the kitchen might help. The inn staff had volunteered to bring in all of our supplies, subverting another turn on the icy parking lot. Maybe my brain needed to see all my tools in their happy places.

"I'm going up to the inn. Gotta recheck the kitchen."

"Have fun. I'm going to chill up in here on this sweet bed with the fireplace going. Are we starting the ginger-bread houses soon?"

"Dough is already in the fridges, chilling. We'll be ready to cut them out later."

Vee nodded her agreement before laying belly down on the bed, one headphone in her ear, the other dangling down the front of her shirt, her fingers going a mile a minute as she messaged with Jon.

I stepped out into freshly fallen snow and gray clouds overhead. Pine trees and aspens crowded my vision in almost every direction. The simple paved pathway from the cabins to the inn was dusted with a confectioner's sugar layer of snowflakes. I felt them falling on my face as I looked up. With one slow, deep breath, I closed my eyes, stretched my arms out, and smiled. This was what Christmas was made of. Snow, the smell of freshly cut pines, and the bite of winter on my cheeks making cocoa taste *so* much better now than any other time of year. Mrs. Davenport was right: being here in the mountains was a thousand times better than celebrating Christmas in the city with all the bustle of everyday. I wondered vaguely if I could work out a deal with the inn to do their Christmas festivities every year. Now, that would be a dream come true.

Clutching my jacket around me and breathing into the multi colored scarf muffling my chin, I started up the walk only to stop in my tracks. Snow sprayed into my hair and dripped down my coat. I'd just been hit with a snowball! With a slow, deliberate turn, I found the person I'd known would be standing there. Some part of me actually wanted to grin at that boyish expression on his face.

"Oh, sorry. I thought you were someone else."

"Nice, Davenport."

"Thanks, I have been known to have a great shot."

"Yeah, I'm sure you have." I turned from him and started walking again, trying to escape another embarrassing exchange with the boss's stepson.

"You didn't ask, you know, Cookie Girl. It's one of your faults."

I turned again, breathing out a long impatient breath that misted into the cold air. "What didn't I ask?"

"Who I was aiming for."

I shrugged. "I don't care."

"But maybe you should," he said. He hadn't stopped walking and was suddenly much closer than I felt comfortable with. I did my best not to notice the way his biceps strained at the material in his long sleeve shirt. Instead, I thought of how ridiculous it was that he probably purposely bought a shirt one size too small to show off his gym membership.

Undeterred, I took a few steps closer to him, looking up into his eyes. It was terribly disconcerting that he held my gaze with an impish smile on his lips. I pointed in the direction of the inn. "In that house are no less than a half dozen gorgeous, improbably thin, and fabulously wealthy spoiled brats just about your same style, Trust Fund. I bet you would find they would be much more interested in hanging on your every word."

I'd made a mistake going closer. I could see it in the way he shifted his stance, leaning closer as the smirk slipped away from his face.

"Maybe I'm not interested in skinny and spoiled," he said.

I shook my head and turned. "Yeah, right."

"You think you know me, Cookie Girl, but you're wrong."

I didn't turn again, but I could hear the crunch of his boots right behind me.

"Don't waste your time trying to convince me of your angelic qualities," I tossed over my shoulder. "You'll have far greater success with your own kind."

"My own kind? What's that supposed to mean?"

I stopped and he almost ran into me, but I was on the attack, and while he hurried to step back he did so with a smile on his face. "Ridiculously rich, self absorbed, and let's see … did I mention obnoxious?" I ticked the qualities off on my fingers.

"That's not very Christmasy of you, Cookie Girl." He grinned, delighted by the color rising in my cheeks. "I thought you were all about bringing holiday cheer."

"I am, Trust Fund. You just delight in making it nearly impossible to do."

"By the way, I don't have one," he said, moving closer. I was close enough to see the way the stubble on his face outlined his strong jaw line and rimmed soft full lips. Ugh! What was I thinking? Stupid pine trees and snowflakes. Stupid romantic cabin. I was seriously losing my mind. This guy was bad news, and I needed to remember it with every stubbly faced smirk he sent my way.

"You're staring, Cookie Girl." He said it low, like he was afraid to speak too loud.

I shook it off, putting a hand on my hip. "Seriously, don't you have someone else to annoy?"

"But you take it so well. I haven't had this much fun since …"

His voice died away mid-sentence, the color draining away from his face at the same time. I stared at him in concern, but before I could ask he just shook his head and started to walk away.

For some reason I didn't want him to. I stood there watching him go, his boots leaving footprints in the snow then being swallowed up by the shadows.

* * *

"So he just froze?" Vee was cutting out gingerbread, and the whole kitchen smelled like the forest from "Hansel and Gretel," only better.

"Just stopped mid-sentence and walked away," I said simply, tucking a blonde strand behind my ear before grabbing the hot pads and pulling a tray from one of the ovens.

"There's something else," Vee said, her knowing glance catching me over the sheets of rolled dough she was cutting. "Spill it."

"There is nothing to spill," I countered, swapping out another pan of house pieces and glancing at the clock on the wall. It was one in the morning.

She straightened, arching herself backwards to counter the hours of bending over the table she'd gone through. The lift in her brows told me she was waiting.

"Fine. You were right about the stubble."

I said it quickly, and very softly, so that she leaned for-ward. "What? Something about stubble?"

"You were right," I said a little more loudly.

"Ooo, that I like even better. I was right about … about the stubble? What? Are you … are you falling for the Davenport kid after all?"

"Falling for? What is this, some kind of Hallmark Christmas Romance? No, I'm not falling for him. The guy makes me want to throw something at his smirky, stubbly face half the time. But … I don't know. For a minute there, he seemed almost human, and I—as a fellow human being—found that slightly attractive. In the most remote, non-sensual way. More as an acknowledgement that I would possibly rescue him if he were bleeding on the roadside, rather than driving by without comment."

Vee chuckled and handed me another pan. I put it into the bottom oven and set the timer.

"This guy is taking you longer than normal. I'm actually kind of hopeful," she said, laying down on the floor. I don't know why, but it looked like the most comfortable place to be, and I had to stop myself from joining her. After the long day of baking it took monumental self restraint.

"My brain can't make what you're saying make sense," I sighed, settling for putting both elbows on the counter and resting one butt cheek on a barstool.

"Did you set the timer? It's all going dark," Vee murmured.

"Yes, the timer is on. Go to the cabin."

"I can't. I'm afraid of the dark, and bears … and possibly skunks more than bears. Have you ever bathed in tomato juice?"

"Ten minutes. We can do this," I said, glancing with bleary eyes at the oven timer. "And no. I usually reserve my tomato juice for drinking."

"It's how you get the stink out," Vee said, raising one hand so I could see the tips of her manicured fingernails extending over the edge of the counter, "and you don't date. You hate boys and then you like them, but you've never hated one like you do Greyson."

"The stink from what?" I couldn't remember what she was talking about. Baking for twelve hours does that to a girl. "I don't hate him, anyway. He just …"

"The skunk spray, you know?"

"Oh yeah. Gotcha."

"How many more minutes," Vee asked.

"Eight. I don't hate guys and then like them. That doesn't make any sense."

"You're afraid of them. I personally blame freshman year."

"Ugh. Please don't bring that up."

"The infamous Bobby F."

"It's too late to talk about old boyfriends, Vee."

"Let me finish." Here, Vee sat up, but I could only see the top of her riotous curls from where I was slowly sinking down onto the counter. "I don't know how you were before him, but after him, good grief. I could hardly get you to go out to dance for a while there."

"He slobbered."

Vee made a face. I could tell by the way her brow crinkled.

"Ugh. Say no more. Ever since him, you've been a hands off kind of girl when it comes to finding true love."

"You forget, I'm not looking. Not that I don't support your efforts. Jon is wonderful. I'm just … not ready for anything like that."

"For kissing?"

"Don't start with the kissing," I warned her, wishing the timer would ring. For the love!

"Look, kissing aside, sometimes you have to let someone in. I can't imagine my life without Jon. It is the most amazing feeling. And that's not just overtired talking. There is such a thing as falling in love with someone who is worth letting the walls down." She was looking at me over the edge of the counter, and I straightened and returned her intensity.

"I believe you, Genevieve. I think you and Jon are great."

She grinned, "We are, aren't we? But I'm not just talking about us. I'm talking about you too. It's going to happen when you think you've got it all under control and then, heaven help us. I've never seen Molly Hayes let loose, and it's going to be a wild one."

Just then, the timer dinged, and thank goodness, because I had nothing left to say.

* * *

"It's a magical little gingerbread village."

"I think we should have cut out a Godzilla and taped a rampage for YouTube."

Vee and I grinned at each other. She had a dribble of frosting on her sparkly jeans, and I was sure there was a smudge somewhere on my cheekbones, but the twenty little houses made of dark brown cookies, all lined and filled with bright white royal icing, looked just like a quiet suburban neighborhood waiting for the festive decorations of the season.

"Next year, for sure," Vee said.

"Girls! These are aaa-mazing." Vanessa grinned, coming into the large gathering room where the houses stood, each one on a glimmering glass cake plate. Vanessa was resplendent in expensive cut jeans, a white and gold knit cashmere, and dangling snowflake earrings.

"Those plates you chose are stunning," I told her, holding a frosting bag in one hand and putting the other on my hip. Mrs. Davenport had special ordered the cut-glass cake plates to be a base for each of the houses. It had a little something to do with the delay in our exit from the city.

"I love that you're delivering these gorgeous little invites by hand. It's the perfect touch. She selected one from the baskets on the counter. Inside a clear sleeve, a sheet of vellum spelled out the request to join the Davenports in the gathering room and bring their gingerbread house to life. That clear sleeve was attached with red baker's twine to a festively decked and plastic wrapped ginger boy or girl, replete with edible beads, raisins and hand piped accents. I couldn't agree more with Vanessa's praise. There was something about a hand delivered invite that said Christmas.

With the deliveries divided between us by floor, Vee and I parted at the elevator with our baskets of invitations.

"Try not to get distracted," she said as the doors slid shut.

The second floor was a breeze. One little girl was so excited, she practically screamed the news to her parents who were still dozing with the blackout shades pulled. I hurried to press the elevator button, anxious to leave the scene of the crime.

When the elevator doors opened again on the third floor, I had to pause and admire before stepping out. The top floor of the inn was smaller, but no less luxurious than the rest of it. The landing was spacious and held the massive Christmas tree we'd decorated in the Davenport family room. I had no idea they'd brought it along. Beneath it, a train chugged around the tracks, weaving through a healthy pile of presents with immaculate bows.

My basket held two final cookie invites. Realizing I was on the Davenport floor put a twang of something I called anxiety in the pit of my stomach. With some trepidation, I knocked on the first door. It swung open moments later, and I stepped back in surprise. Greyson Davenport took up the door frame wearing a towel wrapped low around his hips—and nothing else.

"Merry Christmas." I shoved the cookie into his hand and spun away.

"Hold up, Cookie Girl. Where's the fire?"

"Hopefully not here. You honestly answer the door in your towel?"

"I thought it was Mr. D., okay? Come in, and I'll get dressed."

"What? No! I've got cookies to deliver."

"Oh, really?"

"Yes." I couldn't stop looking at his chest, darn it! It was muscular and broad at the shoulders like he could play football if he wanted to. And the biceps I'd imagined straining at his thermal the day before were just as beautiful in the flesh. No matter where I looked, there was more bare skin. I forced myself to look at his face. It was smirking. Of course.

"Then how come you only have one cookie in your basket?"

"One?" I looked down and sure enough, only one little ginger girl occupied the bottom of my basket. I thought fast.

"I am going to deliver my last cookie and then get some breakfast."

"I have some up here. Omelet, whole grain toast, OJ. I'll share."

"No. Thanks."

"No, you won't eat breakfast or no, you won't eat breakfast with me?"

"No breakfast with you. I draw the line at brunching with …" I waved my hand at him, encompassing everything in the gesture. It was better than trying to describe his bare chest and the towel thing. I walked to the next door and knocked on it. Two little girls opened it, crowding into the space. I loved the expectation in one pair of blue and another pair of brown eyes.

"Hi, Molly," the little one breathed. I remembered her name was Emma.

"Oh, is that for us? Oh, she's enormous!" That was the older one, Jane, taking the cookie into her hands.

"I'll bet you made her yourself. Molly, did you make her?"

"I did." I crouched down and tapped the cookie. "She could use a little home decorating advice. Do you think you two would be free to help her out around ten?"

"Oh, yes," Emma said while Jane nodded solemnly in agreement.

"Good. I'll be down there if you need any pointers."

"Thanks, Molly," Jane said, her voice almost trembling with excitement.

"I like your hair," Emma threw out as the door was closing.

I touched it. It was the same as ever: ponytail with a swoop of bangs that fell into my eyes when I tipped my head, but suddenly it felt special.

"They're right. You have great hair." Greyson was watching me, only this time he had pajama pants on. No shirt, but at least there was something other than a towel girding his loins.

"You forgot something." I pointed to his chest, and he grinned.

"Does this make you uncomfortable, Cookie Girl?"

"No, it makes me think you don't know how to dress without your valet." I started for the elevator.

"You're funny, but I think the real problem is, you're attracted to me."

"Attracted? If you mean I feel a strong urge to act out irrationally when I see your face, then yes."

"No, I mean …" He walked out into the open hallway, meeting me in the middle where I hadn't meant to pause. My intention was to find refuge in the lift before I said or did anything more embarrassing than usual. "I mean you find me irresistible."

"Wrong." I turned and hurried away, clearly unmoved by the smell of his amazing cologne. Wow. That same urge I'd had when I first smelled it passed over me, and I had to remind myself of how awkward sniffing him would be, especially with him forgetting how to put a shirt on. I forced myself to push the elevator button. "If I pass someone selling shirts, I'll send them up. Maybe they can help you remember how to put one on." I mimicked the act of pulling a shirt over my head and sliding my arms in the sleeves for his benefit. His smile deepened as he walked closer, hands in his pockets.

"One of these times, Cookie Girl. You're not going to be able to run, and then what will you do?" He ran a hand through his hair, making a mess of it. I wasn't looking. I was in the elevator repeatedly pushing the ground floor button. My heart was racing like I was being chased, and for once, I felt sure someone would catch me. Only when the floor dinged and the car settled into place did I exhale.

* * *

"You're really leaving?"

"You said I could." Vee looked at me for confirmation, and I smiled brightly to disguise the feeling of anxiety that took hold of me when I thought of pulling off the next day by myself.

"We're watching one of my favorite movies tonight, and I'll have no one to snuggle with."

"I'm sure Emma and Jane will be your movie buddies," Vee said. She had a good point.

I did my best to keep my distance from relationships, but there was something special about those two girls that resisted reservation. Emma and Jane lived for bling, much like their mother. The prospect of crafting houses the day before with every candy imaginable lit up their smiles.

That morning, I had armed them both with a small bag of royal icing and surrounded them with candies of all sizes and shapes. I was surprised to see Greyson slide into his chair nearby with a bored look. Only, he didn't seem bored for long. Candy in and of itself is a generous attraction for most young males, but there was something more. Even though his beginning was halfhearted, he still managed a chimney and some yard décor before the girls noticed his efforts. When they did, there was awed delight over his Lifesaver chimney and candy bar doors. Emma had soon enlisted his aid in recreating his designs on her house.

It only took a pretty smile and wide blue eyes before he had moved to their table and was under Emma's express guidance. Seeing herself fall behind, Jane found me refilling tootsie rolls and asked for my help. She already had a great start. I sank into the chair opposite Greyson so Jane and I could work together. Chocolate squares became roof tiles; wafer cookies became doors; candy covered sunflower seeds became Christmas lights strung on licorice strings; and sliced jelly beans became a rock path.

I had to admit, sitting with Greyson wasn't as awful as I'd imagined it would be. He had a nice laugh, a chuckle at his own humor that went over the girls' heads but still made them giggle along with him. It was impossible not to notice the care he took with Emma, the way he sat her on his lap so she could reach better, and her tender touch of his bearded face when she needed his attention. He was at her service, remarkably gentle and kind as they worked together, his house abandoned with only a chimney, door, and listing snowman. There was something warm and sweet in the way he looked at her when he didn't think I was watching. I could tell that despite his reservations, his affection for these charming little girls was well beyond what he would admit to.

With the final touches complete, we all stepped back. The room was a beehive of activity, laughter, and enjoyment, but our little world fell silent as the girls surveyed their handiwork.

My icicles were way more realistic than his, but both houses were a masterpiece that Jane and Emma could be proud of.

"Do you think Mama will let us bring them upstairs? I want to stare at mine all day long," Emma told Greyson.

"I'll help you smuggle it up there," he said, lifting a cake stand in each hand.

"Careful," I had cautioned, but the girls weren't listening, and he was trailing after them. I watched him go, wondering. Wondering what that snowball attack was really all about. Wondering what it would be like to have a family like Aunt Karen and Uncle Frank. Wondering if I dared to let myself care like that.

Today, I shook off the memory and watched Vee zip up her overnight bag. She was right. Emma and Jane would be more than happy to share a blanket and a tub of caramel popcorn with me as we watched the movie. To top it off, my recipe for caramel corn was hands down amazing. It didn't get brittle when cool but stayed nice, chewy, and addictive. I learned to stay away from it once my portion was consumed.

"You're right. I can now live without you for the night. Go have fun with Jon, but please don't forget me."

"I could never." Vee grabbed me into a hug. Pulling back she whispered, "I promise not to judge you if you kiss that boy."

"Genevieve!"

But she was already waving as she walked out of the cabin, letting in a gust of cold air. That cold air reminded me why I enjoyed my time in the kitchen and that, indeed, I needed to find my way up to the inn. I had a bunch of cookies to bake for tomorrow's frosting. A baker's work was never really done. Cookies didn't make themselves, and it was much different than popping a few in the oven for your own pleasure. My personal recipe for sugar cookies spent several sessions in the refrigerator before ever being taken to the oven. And that was only the beginning. The frosting preparation and coloring took care and precision. With decorating on top of that, I had a full day ahead of me.

It was several hours later, that I hurried back to the cabin to wash up and throw on my new pajama bottoms. Pink and mint green bottoms with embroidered initials for the girls, and blue and gray bottoms for the boys, were a luxurious part of the movie night, courtesy of Mrs. Davenport. In her opinion, the whole point of such an evening was the opportunity to order new pajamas. Decked in my plush nightwear I was ready to be entertained.

The gathering room of the inn was filled with blankets and pillows, places saved on the couches for snuggling, and the flat screen above the fireplace ready for a classic screening of *While You Were Sleeping*. Sandra Bullock and Bill Pullman at their best, dashing from one misunderstanding to the next while falling for each other. I loved watching this movie with my mom, giggling at the drama that developed between the two main characters. The little girl who had snuggled up in her mom's arms found something utterly romantic in the idea of falling for someone when she didn't mean to. Even now, I wished I could feel that way again.

Once the table was set with paper cones of caramel corn, plates of mint cracker cookies, and a delightful Christmas punch, I settled my pillow in the middle of the room. Just as Vee had predicted, Emma and Jane soon found me, their eyes sparkling with delight.

"Mama let us put our ginger houses beside our beds."

"We have our own room because we're too big to sleep with Mama and Papa."

"In the night we can leave on our snowflake night-light."

"I stole one of my candy canes, and ate it."

That was Emma, spoken behind her hand and into my ear. My eyes widened in mock surprise. "Oh no!" Her smile literally split her face.

"Don't worry, I told Mama, but she wasn't mad."

I laughed. "Well, good."

Once the movie began, I was accosted by the two girls and a warm fuzzy blanket. Jane brought over three cones of popcorn, and we got all sticky fingered.

It was strange to me how Greyson kept to the far corner of the room, sunk down low in a chair. He wasn't wearing his pj's, even though everyone received them before coming downstairs. He was wearing a baseball cap pulled down low on his forehead, peeking out from under it as he watched the screen, his arms folded sullenly. No amount of flirting from the girls drew his attention. The movie only received a passing glance.

I could feel his eyes on us as we giggled and shushed one another, but then, somewhere in between the scene where Lucy and Jack slid on the ice and the final credits, he disappeared.

It was well past midnight when I tucked the kitchen in and wrapped a scarf around my face for the short walk by moonlight to my cabin. The air was sharp and cold, the sky remarkably clear. A thousand stars burst above my head, shining with endless abandon as the moon bore down on the snow, taking pleasure in its own reflection. I took slow steps, thinking about the movie and the swell of longing I always felt in my chest when I compared myself to Lucy. I felt so much like her. Alone, and unable to accomplish the dreams of my heart. Six years ago, I'd abandoned the hope of falling for a handsome commuter dropping coins into my booth.

I stopped, staring up at the moon and wondering if it was true what they say, if loved ones really did look down on you from above. I wondered what Mom would say if she knew how broken I was.

I held my breath, hoping something would happen. I wasn't sure what, but I was definitely hoping for a sign. To be honest, I'd been looking for it since the funeral, positive that if ever there were two people who would stay connected, it would be us. But no matter how hard I tried, I couldn't feel her. I couldn't feel anything but the chill creeping in through my boots. There was no shooting star or angelic singing telling me to take up the flame of hope again. There was only the muffled sneeze of a passerby.

Wait. What?

It was after midnight in the mountains with three feet of snow on either side of my path. There were no "passersby".

I turned slowly to look behind me at the inn. All was dark save the light glowing on the wide back porch. Looking back toward my cabin, I wondered if Vee had decided to come back early. A swell of excitement filled my chest at the thought. My steps quickened. But nothing quite prepared me for what was waiting on the steps that were washed gray under the light of the moon. It was hunched, cold, and had excessive facial scruff. Greyson Davenport was waiting for me.

Gingerbread House Dough

Recipe from Christene Houston

  1 ¾ c. flour
  ½ tsp. cinnamon
  ½ tsp. ground ginger
  ½ tsp. salt
  ½ tsp. baking soda
  ½ tsp. ground allspice
  ½ tsp. vanilla
  ½ c. butter or margarine (not oil) softened
  ½ c. firmly packed brown sugar
  Scant ¼ c. molasses (to double, use 1/3 c.)
  1 whole egg

In a medium bowl, mix together flour, cinnamon, ginger, salt, soda, and allspice. In the bowl of your electric mixer, beat vanilla, butter, and sugar for about five minutes–or until mixture is light and fluffy. Mixture will not be completely smooth.

Beat in molasses and egg until blended, and scrape down the sides of the bowl once. Beat in flour mixture on low speed until well blended.

Divide dough into 2 equal parts, and flatten each piece of dough into a circle. Wrap pieces in plastic wrap and refrigerate for at least two hours.

Preheat oven to 350 degrees F. Grease large cookie sheets, or line with parchment paper. If you're making candy windows, please use parchment paper to avoid tragedy.

Once your pans are ready, remove plastic wrap from one piece of dough and place it on a heavily floured surface. Roll out the dough with a thickly floured rolling pin to 1/4 inch thickness. Keep the remaining dough refrigerated until needed.

Use a template and cut by hand or use gingerbread cookie cutters. Using a spatula and a careful hand, place shapes onto the prepared cookie sheets. Bake for ten minutes or until golden brown. Let pieces stand on a wire rack until cooled completely.

I recommend baking the day before you build and letting your pieces cure at room temperature so they're nice and firm for building with.

When you're ready to begin building, make up a batch of Gingerbread House Glue. (Recipe at the end of chapter five).

CHAPTER FIVE

"What are you doing here?"

"You're late, you know?" Greyson's words were slurred. I reached in my purse for the pepper spray I kept there and continued up the walk.

"Not all of us get to walk away from an event without cleaning up, Trust Fund."

"Ah, yes. The life of privilege resented by the working class." Greyson stood unsteadily, placing one hand on his hip in an attempt to look casual.

"Are you aware it's after midnight?"

"Don't worry, I'm not … I'm not going to do anything." He wobbled and then sat down again. His lips were blue.

"You look cold. How long have you been sitting here?"

"A couple minutes," he said dismissively. "Since after the movie."

Two hours by my calculation. "Why, again?"

"You know … I never drank before. I never drank before." His voice faded away and his eyes took on a far off look.

"Did you drink tonight?"

"She loved that movie," he said, running a hand through his hair, "and I just can't think about her without totally losing it."

Something inside me went perfectly still as he said the words. I knew he was revealing something he didn't want to, something he wouldn't share with me if he hadn't drunk away his inhibitions. The words were too close to the pain I knew, and I shied away from them, closing my eyes against the raw brokenness of his smile. I didn't know what to say.

"I've been such a jerk," he laughed, the air coming out in crystal clouds. "I'm sorry."

He raised his eyes at the same time I did. They were that color of blue that catches your breath and holds it. "I don't know how to be nice. When I'm nice it feels like a hot poker stabbing into my chest every single moment of the day. That's why I left." He pounded his chest with each word and tears welled in his eyes, reflecting the brightness of the moon.

He'd really been drinking. I shook my head and stared up at the dark sky for a long moment, trying to unhear the words, trying to unfeel the swell of compassion rising in my chest. I couldn't. I wouldn't.

"Let me take you back to the inn," I said finally.

"That's not my home." He rested his head in both hands. "But I can't go back. If they knew how I blew it … they would hate me."

"Greyson," I held out a hand and he slowly looked at it like he was studying the weave of the gloves on each finger, "take my hand."

"You gonna rescue me, Cookie Girl?"

"Just keep you from loosing your fingers and toes to frostbite," I murmured as I tried to get him onto his feet.

"You should change the name of your shop," he said, standing and wavering dangerously to one side. With a groan, I turned, placing one of his arms around my shoulders and one of mine around his waist. From this perspective the pathway back to the inn looked insufferably long. I had no idea how we would mount the steps, but there was a glimmer of hope that someone would be at the front desk, and I could pass him off to them.

"You have a better idea?"

"Cookie Girl. It's catchy, no?"

"No." I puffed out big clouds of warm air as we walked, and occasionally slid, down the sidewalk. The irony of my favorite scene between Lucy and Jack was not lost on me.

"Why were you out in the snow, anyway?"

"I was waiting for you."

I shot him a look from under his arm before hiking him back up. He was getting heavy.

"Why?"

"You don't show it, you know, but I think you know what it's like." Greyson tried to wipe his nose and almost hit me in the face. I slapped his hand away, and he laughed. "Hey. That wasn't nice."

"Well, neither is dragging a ten ton elephant up the sidewalk, so we're even."

"Am I … am I the elephant or are you?"

Resisting the urge to roll my eyes, I got him to the stairs and wanted to whimper. They looked like twelve flights instead of four steps.

"You're going to have to help here," I told him.

He nodded, trying to look serious. "How many are there. I see eight."

I groaned. "Okay, step."

He laughed and lifted a leg, only to put it down before we reached the step.

"You're killin' me, Greyson," I growled, and he pulled me to a stop. I looked up at him in surprise, and there was a tortured look on his face.

"Don't say that, Molly. Please don't say that."

"I'm sorry. I just need you to focus for a minute, okay?"

"Okay."

Somehow we got up the steps without either of us falling. I leaned him against the wall by the door and pushed it open, hoping to hand him off to Big Ben. Only, from the back door I could only see part of the front desk. What I could see was empty. It was never empty.

"Where are you taking me, anyway?"

"I'm trying to get you in bed." I pulled him back into the crook of my arm, silently cursing my timing. I swung the door open and edged him into the frame, but he pulled me to a stop and turned to look down into my face.

"What did you say?"

"I said I'm trying to get you to your room. Do you have somewhere else you wanted to go?"

"Oh ... I could have sworn there was something about my bed in there." He looked down at me intently, like he was trying to see me clearly. "See, it's right there. I can see it when you don't run away."

"What are you talking about?"

"The sadness. I know what it looks like." He lifted a hand. "Right there." He ran one ice cold finger down my cheek. "I can see where the tears go."

There was something completely unexpected about the way he was looking at me and the touch of his skin on my face. His eyes caught mine, and he touched my chin, lifting it gently. "I'm sorry you cry, Cookie Girl."

For once, I didn't feel the urge to push him away. There was something in his face that drew me in and made me want to hold him close and comfort the pain that was in his eyes. Where it came from, I didn't know, but I did know how it felt to be lost, to be broken and yearning for the peace that could only come from time and healing. All at once, I wanted to know what had broken his heart and why he ran away from it. And somewhere deep inside, I wanted to be the one to help him stop hurting.

But something stopped me. I straightened, looking around the room for a chair. I needed to get rid of this guy, quick. Surely it was good enough karma to rescue an enemy from frostbite, one didn't have to help them to their bed, did they? The nagging in the pit of my stomach told me I knew better, and I propelled my feet through the room. The front desk was even more empty when we passed it and got into the elevator. Inside, I leaned him up against the wall and tried to catch my breath. I needed a moment to get my bearings, to remember why I did not like Greyson Davenport, and to cement my feelings of disdain where they had been earlier, before the moon and the snow and the talking. But Greyson had other ideas.

"I miss her so much."

"Greyson, maybe you shouldn't say anything right now."

He nodded. "I try not to talk about it. I'm hiding from it. Don't tell."

A guilty feeling rose in my throat, and I pushed it down. "We're almost to your room and then you can rest."

His eyebrows rose. "There it is again. You said my room."

"I'm not going to leave you outside to freeze to death," I muttered, "but don't get any ideas."

"Too late," he chuckled, and I was grateful the doors were sliding open to the third floor. Down the hall, I leaned him against his door.

"Think you can get in?"

"What do you know? I remember this place." He placed the side of his face on the door and sighed happily.

"Where's your key, Davenport?"

"Hmm ... which one? The key to my heart or the key to my car?" His eyes were closing. I had a few more minutes before I lost him completely.

"Vee is going to love this." I yanked off my gloves and started poking into each of his pockets.

"What's happening back there," he murmured. "I don't mind, but … wait, Cookie Girl. I want to remember this."

"Just be quiet," I growled, going for his front pocket. Eureka. I found the key card and shoved it into the door slot, turning the handle and just catching Greyson before he fell face first onto the lush carpet of his room.

"Ten more steps."

"That's my bed. Hi, bed. Oh … I missed this place. I feel better already."

I half dragged his body to the bed and pushed him onto it. He fell back and bounced once before settling into the thick comforter. It gathered around his head like a hood.

"I'm an Eskimo."

"You're an idiot. Next time you decide to go for a bender, don't end up at my cabin."

"I don't drink," he said, louder than before.

"Sure. Goodnight, Greyson."

"Molly, wait!"

I turned, swiping blonde hair out of my eyes. "What?"

"I really do love Christmas. I do. That wasn't a lie. But seeing it without her hurts. I just don't know how to love it when she's gone."

I hugged myself. The words could have been mine. They cut into me and left me feeling bare in front of him. I was so grateful he wouldn't remember anything about this night.

"It'll get easier," I lied. "You'll be able to breathe soon."

He stared at me, and for one moment I thought he might be lucid after all. But then he nodded, laying back with one bounce. "You're not a good liar, Cookie Girl."

* * *

I couldn't sleep. Ugh! The ceiling was staring at me. The fire hissed when a wayward snowflake tripped down the chimney; a gust of wind battered against the window and then fled. I tossed once and then lay back, glaring back at the ceiling and wishing I could stop thinking about Greyson Davenport. What was it? Was it the scruff, because seriously, I could not get hung up on that. Was it the way his blue eyes held mine when what I was really trying to do was ignore him, ignore the whole thing about him that made my pulse hum in my veins and kept me looking over my shoulder, hoping and expecting when I shouldn't have been?

I knew better. Loving someone was asking for heartache that could peel me inside out and leave me broken, raw, and ravaged with no hope of making myself right again. It only took a moment, one bad diagnosis, a wrong turn into traffic, a deadly mistake. Everything good came to an end, and with it came a black hole of loss too painful to endure. It sucked the light from the world and left me cold and alone. I'd clawed my way out of that abyss, and I had no intention of going anywhere near it again. So now I would stop thinking about Greyson and his blue eyes and broken heart. I would stop thinking about the way he looked at me, and the touch of his cold fingers on my cheek. I would stop—stop thinking about how he knew my heart was broken, too. Because Greyson was really just a jerk. Yes, I needed to remember that.

I threw a hand over my eyes to stop my brain. To stop it from thinking about the nice things. The battery jump, the way Jane and Emma looked at him, his hand guiding Emma's with a frosting bag, the words "I'm sorry" when I least expected them.

I started to wonder who this girl was. Could she be someone that Greyson was in love with? The thought of Greyson Davenport with his arm around the shoulders of a beautiful girl brought a surprising ache to my chest. It brought me up short and filled me with frustration. What did I care if Greyson's heart was taken? It shouldn't matter to me if he was betrothed since birth.

Most of the night spent itself this way, finally giving in to my pleas for sleep and muting the rage of my brain, until the feeble light of morning crept in and lifted an eyelash.

"I'm up," I moaned. Morning was hateful, especially after a torturous night. I was charged up with cocoa and a granola bar before the sun had wrestled itself from behind the clouds. I decided to ignore my churning brain and defer to the season. Our cabin was too bare. It was obvious we needed a Christmas tree.

I found Ben outside and asked if he would mind me hunting up a pine for my room.

"I'll set an ax and a piece of burlap on your porch in a few minutes. We have a lot of land, just don't stray too far. If you watch the signs you won't go wrong," Big Ben said, pointing up the mountain. I promised to pay heed to postings and went in to finish getting ready. Finding a tree would be a sufficiently distracting adventure for the morning. That left plenty of time for party preparations when I got back. It would involve hiking in snow, an excursion that would leave little energy for thinking about poor little rich boys. Tucking my feet into my warmest boots and shrugging on a thick jacket, I opened the door.

"Hey!"

"Ah!" I jerked back in surprise. It was like *Groundhog Day*, with a sober Greyson. There he was on my porch again. I'd expected him to sleep in after the night he'd had, but no such luck. "What are you doing here?"

"I … I just … I wanted to come say thank you." He looked uncomfortable, and once he started, his words came out rushed. I usually enjoyed his discomfort, but there was something about the slope of his shoulders that had me shrugging as I pulled the door shut behind me.

"Kind act done, you are now relinquished to go about your day of making your stepmom crazy." I gave him a bright smile before turning to lock the door. When I turned back, he hadn't disappeared.

"You're still here."

"Where are you going?"

I looked up at him, debating. "You know, I thought you'd be sleeping in this morning. Don't you think you should?"

"My head is killing me, but I can't sleep," he mumbled, not meeting my eyes. And instantly I knew it wasn't the hangover bothering him. He was thinking about her. The mysterious girl that had spurred his drinking binge the night before.

"I don't usually drink," he added after a long, quiet moment.

"Okay."

"I had no intention of coming to your cabin."

"Good."

He looked up at me and shrugged. "I just thought ..." He didn't say anything after that, and I looked away, fighting the feeling in my throat—the one that wanted to ask questions, to get involved when I knew I shouldn't. I recited my plan in my head. Finish the contract, pay off the van, refurbish the shop, and hang out a shingle. None of it included a handsome young bad-boy with a soft-hearted side. No, I needed him to go away.

"Greyson, forget it. I won't tell Mrs. Davenport if that's what you're worried about. I'm gonna go now, okay?"

"Where?"

I sighed, blowing a flood of steam into the cold air. "You know, I don't think there is a person on the planet more annoying than you are."

He smirked, and the very sight was a relief. "I'm coming."

Eyebrows lifted, I shook my head and backed down the stairs. "No, you're not. I don't take strays."

"I'm not a stray," he said cheerfully. "I can be your sidekick since Vee is gone smooching her lover boy."

I rolled my eyes, wondering how he knew where Vee was, until I remembered how easily they'd hit it off. They were probably besties at this point. It should have been against the law to be friends with your best friend's enemies. As a matter of fact, I'm sure it was. I intended to take this up with Vee when she got back tonight.

"Look, I plan to tromp through the snow searching for the perfect mini Christmas tree for my cabin. I'll probably look at a hundred of them before deciding the first one was just right, after all. Then, I'm going to chop it down and drag it back like a cave woman. So, unless you relish being cold and possibly sap sticky, then you need to go back to the inn and bother someone else."

"I can help, Cookie Girl. Promise, I'll be good."

"Since when has that been in your vocabulary?" I grabbed the ax while he palmed a walkie talkie.

"What's that for?"

"Ben must have left it so you wouldn't get lost." Greyson shrugged, tucking it in his jacket.

"See, there ya go. I'm absolutely fine on my own."

"That's what you say, but think about it, Cookie Girl. Who's going to carry your tree back once you've felled it?"

"Me."

He raised a brow. "I'm good with an ax."

I stepped toward him, tapping the butt of the ax as I spoke. "Video games don't translate well in real life. I learned that when I took tennis lessons. The Wii doesn't actually prepare you for hitting a ball that clears the net. Oh, and you can't play a real electric guitar from your Rock Band practice and have it sound better than a stray cat dying either, FYI."

He rolled his eyes at me. "Just give me the sharp weapon, Cookie Girl."

With a surrendering sigh, I handed it to him. This was such a bad idea.

"Rule number one, no 'Cookie Girl'."

"My rule number one: no rules when hunting for a Christmas tree. This is supposed to be fun, right?"

Another sigh as I turned back toward where the morning sun should be and started walking. We were well into an uphill climb when I heard him start to puff. I could tell his hangover was getting to him, though he didn't complain. There was an overall feeling of calm brought on by the low dark clouds, the feeble light of the sun, and the hush that seemed to be over the world around us. I had a lot of questions I wasn't going to ask, and he seemed to be deep in thought. Finally, he said, "You never said why it's so important to find this tree."

"It's just … a tradition."

"Yeah, we have that one too," he joked. "Is it the one where you tie your underwear to the tree, or the other one where you try to steal and eat all the candy canes before Christmas Eve?"

"Underwear? Really?"

"I was young. Superman was my hero. For some reason I felt the underwear version of him should be up there with Rudolph and Santa."

I shook my head, laughing at the image he painted. Maybe it wouldn't be terrible to share this little part of me. "When I was a girl, my mom would let me make my bed beneath the Christmas tree. All season long we would read stories and make wishes. She would tuck me in under the tree, and I would fall asleep under those multicolored twinkle lights. One year she tried all white lights. We both agreed it just wasn't the same."

"Your mom sounds fun."

"She was," I grinned before catching myself. Dang it. Where was the Greyson who drove me crazy?

"I like falling asleep under the lights, too," he said in between puffs as he neared me.

"Ah, be careful. Your Scroogey façade is slipping."

He laughed, a bark of mirth into the air. "Yeah, you're right."

There were a few trees in this little copse of pines that looked almost right. I closed my eyes trying to imagine each of them in turn. There was a little space in front of the window that would accommodate a tiny tree trimmed in leftover Christmas cookies and strings of popcorn perfectly.

"It's kind of hard to remember." The softness of his voice interrupted the visual image I was conjuring.

"Remember what?" I opened my eyes, startled by how close he was when I did so.

"The reason I started this whole thing. It's hard to re-member who I'm supposed to be anymore."

I studied him carefully, from the ski cap down around his brows, to the scruffy jawline and hunch in his shoulders. His eyes showed he wasn't in his best form. He looked tired. Vulnerable.

"Are you playing a part? I'm guessing the innkeeper or the donk—"

"Don't say it." He shot me a look, and I just laughed.

"Not the donkey, not the innkeeper. More like the prodigal son."

"Ah, but that's a different play altogether. You're not keeping with the Christmas spirit."

"Yeah, well, I haven't felt much of the Christmas spirit … for a long time." Another soft statement, and an exhale that sent mist into the air.

I placed a hand on my hip. "At this point, the only thing that hasn't been done to help you get into the spirit is whacking you upside the head with the Yule log. I'll volunteer to do the whacking if you think it'll help."

"You don't like me." He looked surprised by this thought.

My brows lifted at the look on his face. "You're arrogant and selfish. You make people miserable on purpose and say mean things to complete strangers. I've never met a person more genuinely stuck on themselves in my whole life."

"Just tell me how you really feel," he grumbled, turning away.

"What do you expect, Greyson? You can't treat people like crap and expect them to fall at your feet in adoration. That may work with those rich kids you hang with, but it doesn't work with the lowly common folk who'd rather spit in your cocoa."

"You spit in my cocoa?" He looked incredulously over his shoulder.

"No, but then I'm not *common* either. I'm pretty dang talented at what I do, and I don't appreciate you badmouthing my work."

"I'm sorry, okay?"

"And another … what?" I was just warming up and that little three word sentence stopped me in my tracks. What I couldn't believe was that it had come out of *his* mouth.

"I said, I'm sorry. Did you ever think that just maybe I've wished I could take back everything I said that night?" He had turned around completely, snatching the cap off his head to reveal a mess of tussled hair. His blue eyes blazed as he tromped back through the snow closing the distance between us.

His words crowded into my head and fought with my thoughts. I shoved them aside and said, "That thought never crossed my mind. You haven't said one nice thing about me since we met."

"How do you cuddle up to a cactus?"

"Exactly," I said, my eyes narrowing at the reference I'd used for him only a few days ago, "and just so we're clear, I'm not asking for cuddling."

"Well, maybe you need to."

"What?"

He was coming closer, and I couldn't decide whether to bolt or hold my ground. There was a burning in my chest that kept me from moving away. Something about the look in his eyes made my fingers itch to reach out and touch him. It was the most annoying reaction, but I couldn't shake it.

"Maybe you need to get close to someone for once."

He closed the distance between us with two determined steps, taking up the oxygen in the space around us, bringing out the heat in my cheeks, and leaning in with an intensity that drew me to him. Clenching my hands to keep from giving in to the urge to touch him, I lifted my chin. "I don't know what you're talking about. I'm close to people."

"No, you exist among us, but you hold yourself away, even when what you want more than anything is to be touched." His voice had dropped low again, into a slow rolling rumble that tugged at something in my belly.

"In your dreams, Trust Fund," I breathed. Oh, I'd meant to say it with a sassy little snap, but it came out as more of a gasp because he was still moving closer. How could this mountainside, spread open by white snow and towering trees, feel like a tiny corner I was being closed into? My back met a tree trunk, and he pressed a hand over my head, the heat of his gaze touching my face, my lips.

"My name is Greyson," he growled, chucking the idea of personal space altogether.

"Greyson, what are you doing?"

My words were a plea. A quiet prayer that he would back away and remember the line we danced: the witty banter, the saucy bickering that kept him at arms length.

"Molly." It was a breath with movement, a leaning in with a plea of its own, softly begging for permission. "I'm sorry. I never meant to hurt you, I just … I was angry. They sprung this whole Twelve Days of Christmas on me when I came back to escape it. I struck at everything and everyone, because I didn't know how to handle it. Every day since, I have regretted the way I acted and wondered if there was some way …"

His voice was soft. It tripped to silence as his eyes fell to my mouth.

"Greyson …"

I put a hand up to push him away, but it met with the solid strength of his chest, and instead of pushing it pressed against him, giving in to the surge of desire that rose up inside my chest. His hand found my hip, and a shock wave of fire blazed up from the contact point, igniting a similar blaze beneath the palm pressed to his chest and up my arm. I had no intention of kissing him. I couldn't even be in the same room as he was, for crying out loud. But my brain's intent somehow disconnected from my body's reactions. His hand pressed my body closer to his, the mist of his warm breath filling the air between us. The hand on his chest curled into his shirt, grabbing the edge of his collar and tugging him in. My feet pushed me up on tiptoes, and I realized I'd been studying his lips when my eyes drifted closed, and I met him in the middle.

Gingerbread House Glue
(Royal Icing)

Recipe from Christene Houston

  2 c. confectioner's sugar

  1 egg white

  ¼ t. cream of tartar

Please note: You'll need a very thick frosting. You will get a VERY thick frosting from this recipe. If it is thinner, you will have trouble getting your house to stay together without having to hold it in place for a long time. If you would like your frosting to be a bit thinner, you can play around by adding more egg whites, or sugar, depending on the consistency you want.

Mix all ingredients together until thick and firm. Scoop into frosting bags with a rubber spatula. This recipe will fill one frosting bag very full.

CHAPTER SIX

If I had daydreamed of what it would feel like to kiss the snobbery that was Greyson Davenport, I would have imagined scruffy facial hair assaulting my chin. There would definitely be slobber. Something along the lines of a Guppy wake-up call. But Greyson abolished those imaginary daydreams.

His kiss was soft and gentle, a lullaby to my protests that quietly shushed them to sleep. His strong hands pressed me closer, squeezing out the cold air between us and turning it to fire. My defenses, and all the reasons why this should not be happening, slipped away while my hands traveled his chest, my fingers finding the edge of his jawline and gently exploring the facial scruff that I couldn't handle. It was soft, dang it, and something about it put my temperature through the roof as he nudged the kiss from gentle to urgent. My head was swimming. One of his hands remained on my hip, holding me close, and the other slid up my back to the base of my neck beneath my hair where he could hold me just where he wanted me.

Oh my my.

For a long moment, the sounds of the forest disappeared. All I felt was my heart racing, my blood hot as I moved in closer, letting him deepen the kiss and pull me right against his chest. I could feel his heart beating at a frantic pace beneath my fingertips, the softness of his lips against mine, the sigh I could barely contain rising up in my chest. I was having trouble remembering where we were and why I was trying to push him away. In fact, everything about his kiss was making me think I'd been mistaken all along. Maybe Greyson wasn't a big fat loser with a grudge match for Christmas.

But then I remembered: the cookies, the obnoxious comments, the red flags that told me he was bad news. It restarted my brain, and I pushed instead of pulled. He let me go, and I tried not to wobble as I studied the ground. My lips were on fire. I couldn't seem to form a coherent thought. I grasped onto a thread of indignation, trying to pull it into a cloak around me, to protect myself from the emotion welling up inside of me.

"What the heck, Greyson?" It was more of a croak than an accusation.

"Molly …" He stood back with his hands raised just a little in surrender, and a look on his face somewhere close to shock.

"Don't."

I didn't want him to talk. It was dangerous, the way he was looking at me, and the way my heart was racing. The itch in my fingers hadn't been satisfied by roaming his chest or touching his face. I was staring. Good heavens, what was happening to me? I shook my head, trying to stop my hands from trembling.

"What was that?" Greyson's voice was shaking.

"Nothing. Dang it." I looked down, up, anywhere but at that face, those lips. A huge snowflake hit my cheek and I looked up to see the darkest, most ominous looking cloud directly overhead. I wanted to weep with happiness at the distraction. Yes, crazed snowing was what we needed right now. "Oh, that does not look good."

"Molly, don't walk away."

Snow was the answer. Thick and heavy, covering the awkwardness of this moment, and erasing the footprints that showed how close we'd been. How his boots met mine and melted the snow underneath. I needed to forget what it felt like to touch this man and feel his mouth against mine.

"Greyson, look up." I pointed to the sky. He followed my gesture and stopped, his face changing.

"We have to get back. That doesn't look good."

"I agree."

Greyson pulled the walkie talkie from his pocket, looking like he wanted to say more. I didn't give him the chance. I was already tromping through the snow, bypassing our footprint trail, doing my best to lock away the memories of what happened moments ago.

"Head on in." I could hear a strain of worry in Ben's voice, and I quickened my pace in time with the fall of the flakes around us.

"They're closing down the main road," Greyson said beside me. He'd caught up and we kept pace together even when I started to puff from the exertion. We'd wandered pretty far in our search, and the snow was deeper going back. I could feel my legs begin to burn and almost tipped into a deep pocket. Greyson put an arm around me in just in time, pulling me back onto higher ground.

"Thanks, I was fine," I said, getting away from him as quickly as I could. "Wait, did you say the main road is shut down?"

"Yep."

"But that can't happen. Vee is in the city!"

"She's going to be there for a little while. They'll have trucks up to clear it once the storm passes."

"Which is?"

"Ben said it could be a bad one. They're listening to the forecast. It could be a couple days."

I stopped in my tracks.

"Stop kidding around, Greyson," I said, through a swell of panic in the back of my throat.

I'm grateful for snow plows that have superhuman capacities.

"I'm not kidding. Molly, we're in the mountains. The snow you get in the city is nothing compared to the dump they're prepping for up here." He sighed at the panic on my face. "Don't worry. Mama Lucille and Big Ben have this down to a science."

"How would you know?" I grumbled. Anger surfaced as the most comfortable emotion I could handle at this point, and I grabbed onto it with both hands.

I'm grateful for snow, but not the kind that keeps Vee from me.

"While you've been spreading Christmas cheer, I've spent some time helping Ben. Believe me when I tell you they can handle a little winter storm."

"Lovely. At least one of us is prepared for it. I, on the other hand, have to find a way to entertain a couple dozen people while being snowed in."

"You're freaking out over a little bit of snow? I never took you for a diva." Greyson was beside me again, and I shot him a dark look.

"Because you know me so well."

"What the heck is wrong with you, Cookie Girl?"

"Don't call me that!" I was shouting even though he was standing right next to me.

His jaw flexed like he wanted to shout right back, but he didn't.

"It's going to be okay, Molly. Vee will be up before you know it. They just can't dig out the road while it's still snowing."

The quiet tone he took soothed my nerves even though I didn't want it to. I wanted him to yell. I wanted a reason to shove him away and run in the opposite direction. The emotions blazing around inside my chest were overwhelming. Why did he have to kiss me?

I'm grateful for arguments that make me forget what I'm feeling.

When we reached the cabin I stormed in without saying a word to Greyson, hoping he would go away and leave me alone. He didn't. Instead, he followed me in. "I'll tell her," I heard him say into the walkie talkie.

"Ben and Lucille have a place for you at the inn. They said to bring your gear."

Ugh. Could there be worse news?

I folded my arms over my chest, tipping my chin down and breathing deep.

Grateful for snow even though it's making my life miserable.

Grateful for Christmas trees even though I got distracted and didn't get one.

Grateful for Greyson. No. Not Greyson. Dang it!

I looked up. He was watching me in that relaxed way he had, the one where he leaned back, his legs crossed leisurely, his lean frame reminding me what it felt like to reach out and touch it. The tingling in my fingertips returned, and I clenched them tight, afraid he could read my thoughts or sense my ridiculous fascination with his biceps.

"I'll grab my stuff."

It only took a few minutes to pile my personal belongings into a tote. What took much longer was deciding what we would need for the events ahead of us. Thankfully, most of the essentials were already packed into the kitchen. But there were a few collections that would need to find their way to the inn at some point. I stood in front of the pile in frustrated indecision for a long moment.

"You could talk to me. I might be able to help you decide what you need."

I shook my head. "No thanks."

"Pretend I'm Vee."

I snorted.

"Just relax, girl, you know what to take." He mimicked Vee's sassy style, and I shot him a look. He struck a pose that was so Vee I almost burst out laughing.

"Stop. I'm trying to figure this out."

"You know you want to talk to me." He put a hand on his hip and batted his eyes.

"Greyson, stop it." I was chuckling even as I said it. "Fine. Do I bring up the stuff we had planned for the next two events, or do I leave it since we'll be winging it?"

"Bring what you think you'll need. Maybe you won't use it, but you'll feel better knowing it's on hand."

"It could take a couple trips," I hedged.

"What if we use the burlap to pull it across the snow instead?"

I looked at the stack of boxes before me. Three good sized boxes would fit on the burlap easily, and with both of us pulling we could get it across the snow. Good grief. Why did he have to have good ideas?

The walkie talkie crackled. "Mama Lucille's getting a little ruffled in here. She likes having all her hens in the coop when these storms hit. You kids on your way, or are you hoping to get snowed in at the cabin?"

Ben's voice brought the color out in my cheeks. The very thought of being snowed in with Greyson Davenport made my decision for me.

"Fine, let's do that."

"Just gathering some supplies. Heading up there right now," Greyson told Ben before grabbing a couple boxes and following me out into the snow. The wind had picked up, and the snow was falling faster than I'd ever seen it before. I hurried to lay out the burlap and put the boxes atop it.

"You grab one corner, I'll grab the other," Greyson said. Even walking down the path was arduous in such thick snow, but we made it in good time and stomped our way up onto the porch, shaking our coats free of flakes.

"That wasn't so bad." Greyson looked proud that the idea had worked so well.

I shrugged my bag back onto my shoulder. "Yeah, well, thanks. I appreciate your help. But I hope you'll understand when I ask you to keep what happened on the mountain between us. You're the son of my boss and I don't need any complications."

He looked confused. "Complications?"

"Greyson, unlike you, I need to keep my job."

"You think my stepmom cares who I kiss?"

I winced at the word, and the warm reminder it brought to my belly. "I think it would be better for both of us if we kept our distance."

"Molly, you can't be serious." Greyson took a step closer, but I pushed past him with my bag.

"I am. Just forget it happened. I know I will." Even as I spoke the words, I felt the guilt of being a liar. I just hope he didn't see it.

* * *

The door flew open and Lucille appeared, a pinched look furrowing her brow. "It's about time, you two. Not that I'm scoldin'. Lennox always says I scold other people's kids like they were my own, but I'm not scolding, I'm just—"

"Sorry we took so long. I couldn't decide what to bring from the cabin. We didn't mean to make you worry."

I hugged Lucille, grateful for the way she came between Greyson and I, breaking up the tension that filled the air thicker than the snowflakes falling outside the porch.

Inside, the lobby was a hive of activity. With the threat of losing power, extra blankets and candles had been stacked on the front desk and each couple or family was being delivered their share. Ben stood at the desk with a clipboard in hand while Lucille shepherded us into the room.

"They're here, Ben," Lucille chirped and Ben made a note on his board.

"Thought you two might've gotten distracted," Ben said over the commotion at the counter.

I ducked my head, forcing myself not to look at Greyson, and praying Lucille would think the red that lit up my cheeks was from hiking through the snow, or entering the warm inn, and not the memory of Greyson's soft lips over mine.

"I'll put these in the kitchen," I said to no one in particular.

"I'll help," I heard Greyson say.

"No!" It was too quick and even Lucille's brow raised when she heard it.

"I'll help her, Greyson. I think Ben could use you."

I didn't watch to see his reaction. I was already bolting to the kitchen where I stowed away the goods for the next couple nights.

"We're not meaning to take advantage of your skills, but our cook is stuck on the other side of the mountain. We're hoping to split up the meals between a few of us. Would you be willin' to take a dinner?" Lucille tucked the boxes she held up on a shelf as she spoke.

"Absolutely. I'd love to keep busy," I agreed. The look on her face said she suspected why I might be so eager to help.

"Let's get you settled in your room, then, Molly." She took the back staircase three flights up and paused on the landing of the Davenport floor.

"If we lose power, we'll run the generators for a few hours during the day and night. We have plenty of wood to burn in the fireplaces to keep warm. And plenty of blankets."

I nodded, catching my breath and admiring the Christmas tree that stood there before it hit me. My room was right across from Greyson's. I tried to swallow but nothing happened.

Lucille led the way, offering me a key card once she'd swiped me in. "We'll keep the fire going in the gathering room so if you get cold you can come down."

"Thanks, Lucille."

"Here's a shower rotation list. Different rooms take different times."

"This makes me nervous," I said, taking the paper even as I put my bag down on the white comforter. "I can just see this turning into a game of Clue with the butler in the pantry with a monkey wrench."

"Nothing like a good power outage to inspire the imagination, eh?" Lucille chuckled. "Don't worry. We've had the power out quite a bit and never ended up with a violent butler in the pantry."

"Thanks, Lucille. I don't know why I'm feeling so freaked out." I sank down onto the overstuffed chair and stared at the fire grate.

"Need to talk about something?" Lucille perched on the bench that stood at the foot of the bed.

"I'm just used to having Vee here in case of emergency. I honestly don't know how to throw this party if there isn't power."

Lucille looked thoughtful. "You know, the best times we had as kids up here were when the power went out. Of course, back then, there was less to miss and we were used to being creative with our time. I reckon the same things that entertained us then would entertain us now."

"You're talking about down home folks with an appreciation for the simple life," I said, pushing a lock of hair behind one ear. "I've got a bunch of wealthy people with every bit of new technology and comfort there is to be had. I'm afraid if I suggested toilet paper snowmen they'd turn up their noses and …"

"And what? Walk out the door?" Lucille laughed. "You've got a captive audience, my dear, sometimes the best type to have. Go with your gut. I tell Knox that all the time. Trusting your instincts is what makes you unique."

I gave her a hopeful smile. "You really think it would work?"

"As far as I know, you're the one who has everyone enchanted with Christmas. They can't say enough about you and your talents. Wrap it up in chocolate and whipped cream, and I think you've got them sold." Lucille stood up and smiled down at me. "You remind me so much of my girl. I wish she could meet a nice gentleman like your Greyson."

I tried not to laugh and blush at the same time. "He's not mine. No. Greyson might be perfect for your Lennox, because he's certainly not …"

Lucille winked. "It'll be our secret until you're ready to tell, Miss Molly. But this old lady knows a good match when she sees one."

She turned to go while I gaped.

"Dinner tonight would be so helpful if you can muster it on short notice."

"Of course," I said. At least that's what I think I said. I was too busy forgetting to breathe to know if anything really came out.

* * *

On the back wall of the kitchen hung an enormous black chalkboard. The finish was remarkably smooth and took a chalk marking like silk over skin. Within a few hours, my fingers were white dusted—the side of my hand was, too, from using it as an eraser—as I marked out plans for the night and figured out how much of each item I needed to prepare in order to feed an inn full of people.

Lucille was in and out while I turned on the mixer and added in a yeast mixture with flour and butter. When the dough had come together, I let the rolls rise and stood back surveying the board, grateful the power was holding out. On one side was the plan for the evening – a plan I didn't know if I could pull off, even with Lucille's encouragement. I'd spent a full thirty minutes threatening to melt down with the stress. I'd counted ten gratefuls before realizing I had nothing to lose. It came to me somewhere around: *"I'm grateful for stupid snow and the way it piles into drifts trapping me in an inn full of people who expect miracles."*

At this point, I was going for it, win or lose. Dinner was simple compared to that. Cheesy potato soup took advantage of an enormous bag of farm stand potatoes in the cellar. Salad greens with a poppy seed dressing and crescent rolls painted with butter rounded out the menu. The treats would come later. They would be reindeer-centric for a theme of "reindeer games" once night fell.

Something about being stranded in an old inn at Christmas struck me as incredibly romantic, once I was through panicking. There was nowhere to go, and being surrounded by loved ones or having a favorite person to snuggle the hours away with sounded awfully nice. I shook my head trying to center my thoughts. I'd let them go more lately, daydreaming about what it would be like if I did have a special someone. Maybe my life didn't need to be so lonely. Maybe it would be worth the risk to let someone in, even if there would be inevitable pain in the end.

In the silence, as the yeast worked its magic on the dough and the board stood looking proud of all that was going on, I could hear the wind whistling outside and the window panes rattling on occasion as the snow fell and blew, wrapping us in a shawl of winter white. The quiet usually soothed me but today there was too much of it. In the stillness I found my thoughts wandering. While I stood looking at the board, I didn't see my own hand-writing in chalk, a list of games, a carefully marked down menu, or the hurried diagram of a tablescape. I didn't even see the board. I was lost in memory, reliving the way his hand felt on my hip. The heat of his mouth on mine that defied the snow around us. I remembered how his shirt was feather soft under my fingertips and the planes of his chest firm beneath it. Most of all I remembered the feeling of the world around us holding its breath, the col-lective hush that enfolded us and didn't seem to notice me pulling Greyson much closer than I should have been.

Gah!

I'd told him I would forget it, and here I was needing to fan myself when the world was below zero outside.

I shook my hands out and rolled my shoulders. I'm done with that.

Greyson walked in the room and I rolled my eyes.

Could the timing be any better? Universe? I'm talking to you.

"Daydreaming about me?"

There it was. Annoying and yet horribly endearing. What was happening to me? The things I'd found easy to hate were slowly becoming the things I enjoyed most about this man. That was dangerous.

"I have a few more important things to think about than you, Trust Fund." I motioned to the board I'd been looking at. "I'm feeding an inn full of people and planning a new party on the fly. I think my brain can do more than think about kissing."

"So can mine, I just choose not to." He grinned, walking in to stand next to me. He looked at the board critically. "Cheesy potato soup, homemade crescents, poppy seed dressing …" His stomach audibly growled and I turned to look at him.

"Your stomach seems to think it's a great plan."

"My stomach is often rebellious, but this time, it's right on."

Narrowed eyes popped open in surprise. "Wait for it …"

"Wait for what? I told you before I was sorry about being such a jerk. I really am. I'm … turning over a new leaf."

"Why?" I asked.

"Because, it's Christmas." Greyson smiled that smile I'd been ignoring since the day I met him, and I felt my resolve wobbling.

"Greyson, don't do this because of what happened out there. I told you—"

"I know. I know, you've forgotten all about it, though you do blush amazingly well, Miss Hayes. I'm not … being a better person because of you. I'm doing it for—"

"Ah, there you are. Greyson, thank you for volunteering to help our Molly. She's got quite the evening ahead of her. I always tell my girls, 'Many hands make light work.' " Lucille had broken in at just the right moment. I stepped away from Greyson and tried not to look at him as she studied us together. I didn't want her getting any other romantic ideas.

"At your service, Mama Lucille." Greyson was the epitome of charm. I kept looking at him in spite of myself, wondering what had exacted this change in his demeanor. Maybe he wasn't completely sober.

"Have you been drinking?"

I whispered it under my breath while Lucille opened the fridge and pointed out a few things we might need.

"No, why?"

"You're being nice. Like … normal."

He raised a brow at me. "And I can't be nice *and* sober?"

"Um, you haven't been since I met you."

"You're never going to let that go, are you?"

"I don't have a reason to," I said, placing the other hand on my hip. I didn't realize I'd turned away from Lucille and was facing Greyson.

"I said I'm sorry," he said, looking into my eyes. That was such a mistake. There was something about his eyes that spoke to mine no matter what his words were saying. It happened that first time when he caught me off guard at the Davenport house, and it happened now too. I felt like he could see me, truly, when he looked into my eyes. There were things there I wasn't ready to show him.

"Fine. You're sorry. I just didn't know it meant you were going to become a completely different person."

"That's just it, Molly. I was a different person when I was acting like that. I never got the chance to tell you that. I wanted to explain, but—"

"You don't need to, Greyson. I accept that you're a nice person under all that angst."

He took my hand and I wanted to snatch it back. I threw a glance to Lucille, but she was gone. Oh no! So much for trying to convince her Greyson and I weren't an item.

"Greyson, please. I have a lot to do."

"I can work and talk at the same time," he said confidently.

I wanted him out of the kitchen. Where was Vee when I needed her? This was not going to work. Because the longer he stood there looking at me, the easier it was to look back. The longer he spoke, the easier it was to listen. The longer he breathed, the more I cared, and I knew this was not going to end pretty.

"You have to peel and talk."

"Deal." Greyson smiled, and this time it lit up his face in a way that was becoming more common with every grin.

I tossed him an apron and then a peeler. He held them up. "I know what to do with this, but I'm not so sure about this." It was the apron.

"Okay, pretty boy, I'm glad you know how to use the peeler, but I can't have you ruining your fancy clothes now, can I?"

I walked toward him, holding my hand out for the apron. To be fair, it was frilly, but just around the top of the bib. I took it and held up the loop for his head. "All right, in you go."

He dipped his head and I slipped it over, coming much closer than I'd intended. I caught my breath and he stepped in further, placing one hand on my hip. "Molly, I'm sorry I was such a jerk when we met. I said it before, but I don't think I said it how it needed to be said."

I dared to look up into his eyes. They were so blue I felt a twinge of mourning that I'd lost time staring at them. Looking down, I stepped back and around so I could tie the strings behind him.

"Thank you, for saying that." I held up a potato. "We need this whole bag peeled."

"As you wish." He grinned, and there was a sparkle in his eyes.

I turned back to the fridge and rummaged around for carrots, celery, and cheese. With another peeler in hand, I stood beside him at the counter. He was already several potatoes in. "Woah, don't tell me you're some kind expert potato peeler."

"Nah, nothing like that. My grandma loves to cook, and I was her assistant. You would have thought my sister …" He paused, and I looked up from the carrot I was skinning to study his face. There it was again, the feeling of loss that came when he said that word. Sister. He swallowed and then continued. "My sister was more interested in helping Grandpa on the tractor. I spent a lot of time shucking peas, coring apples, and peeling potatoes."

"Your grandparents? Did you visit them a lot?" See, I could do this. It didn't mean anything. I could handle it.

"I lived with them after my parents' divorce."

Picking up another carrot, I began to peel as I put together the story he was telling. "How old were you?"

"I was seven and Rosie was five. We spent almost our entire childhoods on my grandparents' farm in a little town outside of the city. I milked cows and learned how to drive a tractor."

I could not believe my ears. Vee would be delighted to know she was right from the start about his farm-boy physique. I chuckled to myself, and Greyson looked up.

"What?"

Shaking my head, I chose another carrot. "Vee has this knack for knowing things about people. It's how she got to know me. I don't have a lot of friends, but she walked in and it was like she knew my story before I told it. It was horrible."

"Horrible? But she's your best friend."

I looked at him sadly. "Yeah, I know."

"I don't get it."

I sighed and peeled more determinedly. "It's easier if you don't get attached, you know? Everything ends, and being close to someone just makes it hurt more."

He was quiet for a long moment, and I felt certain I'd said the words that would silence him forever. They were deep words from a very painful place in my heart. They were the reason I pushed people away, the basis for every night I spent at home. Because yes, being lonely was hard, but loving someone and losing them … that was harder. That was hell.

"I totally get that," he said finally, looking at me. He stopped peeling and leaned on the counter, as though he needed its support. "I totally get it."

I shot him a look and then grabbed all the carrots and dropped them into the island sink. He brought over a pile of potatoes to join them, rinsing his hands under the running water before looking at me. "Is that why you try to keep everyone at arm's length, because it feels easier?"

I studied the running water wishing he would stop asking questions. The way he asked them without judgment made me want to let him know that part of me I kept hidden away. If he knew how broken I was, would he still look at me the way he did when he kissed me? And could I bear to let him?

"It's easier," I said finally.

"Easier than …"

I looked away, wincing. It hurt to talk about stuff like this. It hurt to say the words. I could still feel the ridge of the scars in my heart. They hurt when I breathed too deeply, when my heart swelled too far with emotion, when I felt too much. I searched for a way to break the tension, to ease away from the pain.

"Greyson, I don't even know you." He pushed himself away from the counter and nodded slowly.

"You're right. Maybe we should start with introductions."

I glanced at him, and my brows lifted curiously.

"Introductions?"

"Hi, my name is Greyson Davenport." He stuck out his hand, the one he'd had on my hip earlier, but I ignored it.

I shook my head. "Yep, already up to speed on that one, Trust Fund."

"And I don't have a trust fund—at least I don't think I do."

"Trust me, you do," I laughed.

He chuckled too, leaning a hip against the counter. "I grew up in a small town doing farm chores and being my grandma's sous-chef. I refused visits with my dad until they were no longer required as an adult, and even then —holidays wouldn't be the same without my grandparents and sister."

I watched him because I could see the shadow moving over his face. The laughter died and his smile slowly wilted.

"I'd been living away at school for the most part, but I came home as often as I could. I left for good when my sister died. I'd like to say I was growing up, getting out on my own, but I felt more like a five year old running away." This time his laugh was mirthless. It was derisive, chiding himself. "I worked wherever I could for the first year, but when I went home for that first Christmas it was … intense. I don't really remember much about it, other than a suffocating feeling of barely surviving. After that, I walked away and didn't look back. I kept in touch in the barest sense of the word. I've barely talked to my grandparents in the last twelve months.

"My dad always seemed to live a carefree life. A life without worries, without caring about anyone or anything. A life without remembering. After a particularly horrible breakup this summer, I decided that maybe it was time to take him up on his offer. It took me until December to work up the courage to become a Davenport."

His eyes slowly lifted to mine, and my heart caught. There it was, the truth behind the mask. It was brokenness and bleeding. I couldn't hold his gaze for long before I looked away.

"It's been tough from the start. If I thought I was running away from my past, I was so wrong. Somehow, my history kept showing up. I made a grave mistake and mentioned my childhood love of Christmas to Vanessa. This whole extravaganza is the result of that passing comment. If I was back home I would have been given a homemade stocking. Here I get a new wardrobe, the keys to a fast car and enough parties posh enough for the Queen. I've never seen so many sparkling lights and fancy cookies. No offense."

"None taken."

I started to cut potatoes while he spoke, needing the effort of keeping my hands moving to still the racing of my heart. His words felt heavy, weighed down by the truth they carried.

"I kind of miss it. The simplicity of home." He paused, looking into the distance, and then said quietly, "Who am I kidding? I miss everything about it."

"Then why not go back? You obviously don't love your dad's home—or even his family."

"I've been such a loser about that," he moaned, slowly wiping his hands down his face. "Good grief, I've been a jerk about everything. Vanessa—she's really kind of nice, and you've seen how amazing those little girls are. I did my best not to like them, but I'm hopeless." He paced back to the other side of me and started peeling potatoes again. The sound of the peeler shucking away the skin of the potato and my knife hitting the cutting board was all that filled the silence between us for a long moment.

"My whole goal in coming here was to stop feeling, to hide behind this mask of being the rich guy who didn't care. And I didn't. I didn't care about my dad or his money. I didn't care about Vanessa or the girls. I thought shutting down was the answer. But it didn't work."

I looked over at him, and I couldn't handle the look on his face. There was a depth of pain I had seen before, an aching that went so deep it made it hard to breathe. That itching in my fingers happened again, the need to touch him, to shelter him from the pain I knew too well. There was a struggle raging inside of me. One side wanted to hide, to turn away from him or say a flippant comment that would preserve the wall I had so carefully crafted between us. The other longed to give in. To give in to the side of me that wanted to comfort him, to understand the different Greysons I knew, and to find out if the man I kissed on the mountain was the one who would be sticking around. The war went on in my chest as I filled a pot with water and vegetables and put it on the stove. As the flames jumped to life I had the same urge to jump. To leap without looking back, without counting the cost. Wiping my hands, I approached him. He watched me coming, his face open. I felt like he knew the battle too well.

"Greyson, I don't usually do this. It freaks me out to get close to people. And you telling me this, about your family, it scares me to want to know. I've gotten pretty good at building walls—it's just my thing." I stopped, not sure how to continue. Words seemed to get all mixed up in my head and sound ridiculous when I thought about speaking them. Instead, I leaned against the counter beside him and looked up into his eyes. "I'm listening."

His smile, that one I'd been avoiding for a while, slowly dawned on his face. He turned and rested his back against the counter, and I moved close enough that our arms were touching. Carefully, he wove his hand under mine. I let him. As easy as that sounds, it was monumental for me. To let him hold my hand, to touch my arm to his, to accept his closeness. It was huge.

We both looked down at our hands. Mine were clean and pink from washing potatoes, and his were warm and rough on the insides, another testament that he had not always lived a cushy life.

"My sister …" He paused, and I felt him struggle to go on. Gently, I wrapped my other arm around his and leaned my head against him, hoping the strength I had would somehow seep through to him just from touching. He took a deep breath and chuckled a little.

"It never gets easier, talking about her. I'm always afraid of what people will think."

"You don't have to worry about me judging her. Say what you need to say. I'm just listening."

He put his other hand over mine and sighed. "My sister, Rosie … she committed suicide two years ago."

I gasped despite thinking I was prepared. And then I sank into him, melting into his side with the weight of sorrow I felt almost instantly. I didn't know what to say.

"In one moment, the girl I knew, the one I protected and fought for … fought with, was gone. I've never been angrier than when she left me."

"Greyson, I'm so sorry."

Those whispered words sounded like an egg with the insides carved out. Empty and fragile and not much good to anyone. I knew how it felt to hear them and know that they could not ease the pain or extinguish the hurt that raged within. I felt him tremble and gasp, trying to hold in the tears. Without thinking, I turned, straddling his legs and sliding my arms up and around his back, sinking against him, my head on his chest—all of me there ready to buffer his pain, soak it in, swallow it down, and bear it just a little.

His forehead sank down on my shoulder, and his arms enveloped me. A gasping sob, a broken whimper, and then, "Everyday I wonder what I could have done. I did everything I could to protect her, but it wasn't enough. It wasn't enough to save her.

"Sometimes it feels like a terrible secret trapped inside of me. When I tell people how she died, I can see the change in their eyes. I see the judgment. But she wasn't crazy. She was amazing. She was the best person I've ever met. Every day without her feels like a hole in my chest I can't begin to fill."

I nodded, understanding.

"So you don't fill it," I said into his shirt, my voice a whisper. "You just walk around empty and hurting and wishing there was a way to breathe without the pain."

"Yeah."

I looked up into his face, stained with tears, broken and just so beautiful. Touching his cheek, his chin, and then pressing a hand to his chest, I felt like I was seeing him for the first time. That first day, I'd noticed a bunch of hair and sharp blue eyes. I'd noticed a nicely built frame. I hadn't noticed the little wrinkles around his eyes that said he once laughed a lot. I didn't notice the way the shadows crossed his face when he thought of her, this girl he loved so much. I didn't notice the pain behind the façade of banter. But I saw it now. I saw a man who missed someone. Someone who could never come back and fill the emptiness they created.

"Greyson, I'm so sorry."

"People say that a lot," he whispered, looking down at me with an intensity that stole my breath away, "but I think you're the only one who knows how to mean it."

Those words sank into my heart, pulling me back into his arms, and I listened like only another grieving soul can.

"My grandparents said it wasn't my fault," Greyson said. "But how could I not have noticed? How could I not see that she was so desperate? That's all I could think about afterwards. Maybe if I had been a better brother, she would still be here."

I shook my head against him, pushing back and sliding my hands down his arms until they cradled his hands. Sniffing, I looked up into the bright blue eyes.

"Do you really think so?"

"I was so busy, Molly. I was dating this girl and going to school, finishing up my degree. We used to talk all the time. I would come home and see her paintings. She struggled with this element of her personality that we never quite understood. Grandma would fight with her all the time about getting counseling, about seeing a doctor for meds, but she didn't want it to affect her painting. She told me once that in her darkest moments she created the most beautiful things. Even though it scared her, there was a part of her that couldn't let it go, that couldn't be without it. I don't think she even knew how bad it was until it was too late. Until she couldn't see the light anymore."

"Greyson, I can't imagine how you must have felt. She sounds like a beautiful person. I wish I could have known her."

"Maybe if I hadn't been so caught up in this ridiculous life, I would have noticed. The signs are all there when I look back. When she started back at the university, we went months without talking. Her roommates said she was hiding out more, not coming out of her room like she usually did. There was something in her voice when I talked to her last. I can still remember it, Molly. It's a pounding in my brain that never lets up. If only I had gone to see her, taken some time to talk to her, maybe she wouldn't have felt so hopeless. Maybe we could have convinced her to take the meds. Maybe she would still be here."

There was a long silence, a stretching of time between us while I battled my own fears, beating them back and then letting them consume me, only to push them away again. The look on his face, the sheer agony of his confession made me bold, thrusting aside my fears and planting the words on my tongue.

"Greyson, I don't know what your sister was experiencing. I don't know what she must have been feeling, but I know what it's like to live in the dark. My depression ... I think it was different. Maybe Rosie's was chemical while mine was situational. When my mother died ..." I stopped, catching my breath on the words. It's amazing how they still cut when they left my mouth, stirring up the pain that laid in my chest under a blanket of gratitudes.

Closing my eyes, I thought through a couple of things I was grateful for.

I'm grateful that Greyson is brave enough to share his story with me.

I'm grateful that I want to share mine, even though it hurts.

"I don't ever talk about this," I whispered.

He touched my face, tucking a stray wisp of golden hair behind my ear. "You don't have to, Molly."

"Yeah, I kind of do. Because you're standing here thinking ... thinking it was you and I just can't let you go on like that." I took a deep breath and closed my eyes.

"When my mom died, I fell into a blackness I'd never known before. It was like this great horrible beast unfurling itself in my chest, dampening out every spot of light, every ray of hope, silencing the voice I had known." I opened my eyes and looked into his. "It was the most frightening place I've ever been. I was surrounded by people who loved me, who did everything they could to find me inside my darkness—but for me, there was a long walk I had to take alone before I could hear them calling out to me. I don't know what it was like for Rosie because we all experience depression differently, but I'd like to hope she knew you loved her. And I'd like to think she would want you to be a champion for yourself like you were for her. The last thing she would want is for you to become someone you're not, to punish yourself like this."

He chuckled a little and looked away. "I want to believe you."

"But you don't know how?"

He shrugged, "What if I haven't suffered enough?"

"What if you have?"

He looked at me again, his eyes tormented.

"What if you have done enough running away, and now it's time to let someone help you find the light again? What if it's time you lived your life *for* her instead of regretting it?"

I bit my lip even as the words left my mouth, hoping I wasn't hurting the tender parts of his soul that were still bleeding and in so much pain.

He straightened, drawing fingers through his beard and walking toward the door. He turned back. "I just … I just need a minute."

I nodded as he left the room.

I watched him go, a sinking feeling in my stomach. Slowly, without prompting I started to think it.

I'm grateful... It took a long moment to find the light this time.

I'm grateful for words that come out and break your heart.

I'm grateful that I wasn't afraid to speak them.

Cheesy Potato Soup

Recipe from Christene Houston

6 large potatoes, peeled and diced

3 stalks celery, diced

2 large carrots, peeled and diced

1 medium zucchini, diced

6 chicken bouillon cubes

White Sauce:

¾ c. butter

¾ c. flour

1 quart (approx.) milk

1 c. shredded cheddar cheese

Combine potatoes, celery, carrots, zucchini, and chicken bouillon in a large stock pot. Barely cover with water and boil until soft. *Do not drain.* Once softened, mash with a potato masher.

Meanwhile, in another large pot, melt butter. Remove from heat and gradually whisk in flour until smooth. Gradually whisk in milk until combined.

Return to heat and add cheese, stirring until cheese is melted and sauce is thickened.

Finally, combine the two pots together and enjoy a delicious soup with homemade bread if desired.

CHAPTER SEVEN

The rolls were just out of the oven, clothed in a sweater of melted butter; the soup was murmuring on the stove top; and I was leaning against the counter when he walked back in. The apron was in his hands. He held it up in surrender.

"Still need a hand?"

I shrugged, motioning to the stove. "Hungry?"

He nodded, still watching me. "Painfully."

I grabbed two bowls from the counter and filled them with hot soup. With rolls perched on top, I returned to where he stood and held one bowl out.

He took it, dunking a corner of the roll into the soup and taking a bite. I used the edge of my spoon to ferry a few bites to my lips before stirring the creamy soup in concentric circles as I spoke.

"I sometimes say things—"

"Stop right there."

I looked up at him in surprise, unsure what his next words would be.

"You think I'm mad?"

I closed my mouth and looked at him questioningly.

He put his bowl down and walked to me. "Thank you for what you said. It's not like no one has ever told me those things. My grandparents tried to make me hear the same words, but I wasn't ready. I didn't think I was ready today. But when I walked away, instead of hearing Rosie's voice the last time I talked to her, I heard yours resounding in my head. And for the first time since her death, I could see her smile. I haven't been able to remember it for a long time. I got stuck on the way she looked when we laid her in that coffin. But that wasn't her. So thank you."

"You're welcome."

He nodded, leaning back against the counter and picking up his bowl. Snowflakes beat themselves against the window and the soup warmed me up from the inside out. But in the silence I could hear his questions. They weren't shouting. They were standing quietly, queued up, waiting to be addressed. Ignoring them only made me feel like a jerk.

"You want to know, don't you?"

He looked up innocently. "If you feel like talking."

"I don't." I sighed. "It's so hard for me to talk about this stuff, because I wish it had never happened. I look back and I think that maybe if I had been a better person I wouldn't have fallen so hard."

His eyes, I swear they spoke before his mouth did. How did I miss that for so long? They said I was safe and that he wanted to see this side of me that wasn't picture perfect.

"What happened, Molly?"

I pushed my bowl away, wrapping my arms around myself again, wishing I could walk away from this conversation, wanting to escape the sting that always came with revisiting that dark time in my life. But he didn't let me hide inside myself. He put his bowl down and extended his hand. I looked at it uncertainly, finally reaching out and taking it. He pulled me close, leaning against the counter and putting a hand on each of my hips. With his touch grounding me, I felt brave enough to begin.

"My name is Molly Hayes and my mom died of cancer."

After a long pause of trying to make the words come out, I finally managed. "It started out as a little dot. She showed me the films. This tiny little dot that looked so harmless. As a kid, you think your mom can do anything. She was more than a superhero to me. She was my everything. I only knew it was serious when she stopped getting up and making breakfast. She loved to cook. But at one point, the most she could muster was to move from the bed to the couch. And sometimes she just stayed there in her pajamas for days. She fought it like a dragon. And we thought we beat it."

"How long ago?"

"Six years this summer."

I stared at the pattern of the old tile on the floor, "We thought she was getting better and then, just like that, she was gone. I was sixteen and needing her so desperately. One minute we were planning a cruise to Alaska to celebrate. It was kind of like this bucket list she came up with and I was her sidekick. We were the *Gilmore Girls*. She was my Loralai and I was her Rory. We did everything together. We got each other. Even when she was sick, she would have me come and lay on the couch next to her and tell her everything I'd done that day. When she couldn't get up much, I would read to her and we would talk about our favorite characters."

I raised my eyes to his for just a moment, glancing off the compassion I saw there. Something about it made me feel more fragile, but I took a deep breath and remembered I was grateful for the sound of her voice when she laughed. I had to work hard to control my voice before I started again.

"When she left me the world I knew crumbled. I had to move out of our apartment, all her things were boxed up, everything about the life we lived seemed to vanish before my eyes. It was like melting snow on a hot day, and I tried everything to feel her presence, to know she was still with me, but I didn't feel anything."

Wiping my nose I folded my arms around myself. "I hate talking about this."

"I'm sorry. We can stop if you want."

I shook my head. "You're right about feeling like it's some kind of horrible secret. No one wants to talk about depression. After Mom died, I fell into this darkness that felt neverending. I would wake up so exhausted from the act of opening my eyes, I couldn't get out of bed. After school, I would come home and sink into my bed again without having spoken one word all day long. Not one. It wasn't like there weren't people who cared about me, but I couldn't feel anything but pain. It was raw and constant and aching in a way I can't even describe."

"I know," he said softly. "I know exactly what you mean."

I dared to look at him and felt almost sure he did know. Hmm. I'd never considered that before. That someone else knew what I felt like.

"Well, falling into depression is a heck of a lot easier than clawing your way out. Overnight, I went from optimistic hope to desperate despair. There was nothing I could do to shake it. I couldn't think myself better. The darkness just overpowered me. So many days would find me on the floor crying without the strength to get up again. I was just … broken."

"What happened?"

I shrugged. "Nothing. For a long time there was nothing but mourning to be done. I got through that school year, my senior year, by the grace of God and my good grades in years past.

"Six months into it, my Aunt got mad enough and I finally told her how bad it was. She took me to a doctor, and I got some meds that helped me chase the darkness. I know that sounds so weak …"

"Why do you think that?"

"Because, Greyson. If I had diabetes or a broken arm, people would get it. They would understand why being on a daily regimen was necessary for me for a while. They would applaud me for my self care and being in tune with my body. But because I struggled with depression, this hidden illness that shows up in the shadows and doesn't scar the outside of my body, I feel like I'm a failure somehow. Maybe if I was stronger or better or smarter, I would be happy without that little pill, but I wasn't. Not for a long time."

"What about now?"

I smiled slowly. "You're going to think I'm crazy."

He shifted my hips close so that I moved toward him. "You forget who you're talking to."

"This is different."

"Then I'll have something to heckle *you* about."

I lowered my head. "I do this thing … I think about the things I'm grateful for."

"Grateful for?"

"I know it sounds stupid, but Aunt Karen suggested it after reading this study on the effects of gratitude on the mind. I wanted to get off the meds if I could. I felt like I was through the worst of it, and I'd been okay for a while. But I was scared of the darkness, worried it would come back without that little pill. She told me to think of something I was grateful for anytime I started to feel that anxiety sinking in. I talked to my doctor, and with his help we slowly backed off the meds. I started being grateful. Ugh, that sounds like Mary Poppins."

"Stop it. I don't know why you think that."

"No one solves their problems by being thankful," I muttered.

"You did."

I nodded. "I did. It doesn't keep me from being sad but it's become this reactive choice to see things differently, to focus away from my fears. I just—it works for me. Maybe there will be a time when I need medication again. I'm not afraid of it like I was before. I know it can work, and I am so thankful for what it did for me. But as long as I can, I'm going to use this method to balance my fears."

"That's incredible." Greyson looked down into my face, his face thoughtful and something else that made my heart race. "Thank you for telling me this. Rosie didn't like to talk about it. It was hard for her to find the words to explain how she felt and what it was that pulled her away from us. Sometimes she said she tried to ignore it and pretend like things were normal. I think she thought she was flawed in some way and she had to ignore that part of her. I wish I knew the way to make her see how extraordinary she was."

"You sound like you were a good brother."

"I'm trying to believe I was. I know I could have done more."

I nodded. "The plight of every human is the regret we feel when we miss the boat. When we look back and wish we had seen clearly what seems so vivid now. For a long time I could only see the sadness and loss. I forgot the beautiful times, the happy memories and laughter that filled our lives. I don't think she would want you to forget that."

He nodded, looking up at the ceiling. "She used to make me sit for her."

I cocked an eyebrow.

"She would make me hold fruit or flex my biceps so she could work on musculature."

"You were a male model?"

"Don't get any ideas. I was covered. And she heckled while she painted. That's why I grew this." He rubbed at his facial hair. "She was always making fun of the peach fuzz I had in high school."

"If she could only see you now," I chuckled.

"Yeah. I hope she would be proud."

"I hope my mom would be too."

He was quiet, looking at me. "This is just what I needed. Thank you."

I grinned. "Yeah. It was nice."

"What do you need?"

I looked up at him and then away. "Nothing. I got through baking school. I started my own business. I'm opening a bakery next year thanks to you and your 'love of Christmas.' " I put the last three words in air quotes.

"That's remarkable. I finished my bachelor's the year before Rosie died."

"What did you study?"

"General contracting," he said. "I could help you get your bakery up and running if you want."

"No."

I said it too quickly and hastened to amend. "Thank you. Greyson, thank you for telling me your story and for turning out to be a decent person instead of … the person I thought you were before. I'm really glad. But, after this," I motioned around the kitchen where the festivities awaited for the night ahead, "I'm going my way and you can go yours. No attachments." Even as I said the words they felt hollow.

"Are you serious?"

"I don't get attached. It's just my thing. It's a decision I made a long time ago and it works for me. I'm better off alone."

"Really? Because I don't see you as being alone."

"Look, Vee is her own force. I don't get to tell her to go away. I've tried, believe me. And Karen and Frank and the kids, they're my guilty pleasure. I know I'll pay for it, but I can't just let them go after all they've done for me."

"But everyone else? You're willing to be alone for the rest of your life?"

"I can't risk it, Greyson. I got out last time, but I don't know if I could ever do it again. I don't know if there is any amount of being thankful or pills or hoping that could get me up off the floor again. So I don't chance it. I don't let myself fall."

I stepped back from him then, and he let his hands fall to his sides, his head bowing in thought.

"I understand."

I nodded feeling oddly disappointed at his words.

"I get it," he said again. "That means I understand where you're coming from, but it doesn't mean I won't try to change your mind."

* * *

That evening settled in like a warm blanket: cozy, inviting, and toasty around the fire. In the large gathering room, families and couples grouped together to participate in various activities while I brought in supplies for the fun ahead. Greyson watched me from the corner of the room. Emma nudged him with her elbow whenever it was his turn to play. After finally losing at whatever game they were playing, he found a way out of the next round and walked over to where I was setting up a table of goodies.

"Do you ever run out of delicious things?"

"Nope." I settled three tiny square plates of peppermint bark down the middle of the table right next to some marshmallows dipped in chocolate and graham crumbs and stuck with striped paper straws.

"I'm willing to help you in any way," he said after trying to snitch a piece of bark and getting his hand slapped, "including, but not restricted to, food testing."

"You're so self-sacrificing."

"I know, right? You didn't know I would do that for my family did you?"

"Let's be honest, before today I didn't know you even liked your family."

"And now you know my true character." He smirked, and I tried to remember how offensive I had once found that expression, with little success. This was not going to be easy.

"Now, I don't know what to think," I said, turning to the cake plates where a foam cone—adorned with red, green, and powdered sugar donut holes—stood. I made sure none of the holes were loose from their toothpicks and then stepped back to eye the presentation.

I'd commandeered the huge chalkboard from the kitchen and had placed it behind the table. In flourishing chalkboard script, that included lots of shading and artistry, I'd drawn the words: "Reindeer Games." On the table below there was peppermint bark, reindeer cookies, reindeer poop (mini malted milk balls) in tiny cups, and reindeer cupcakes. There were dipped marshmallows and donut holes, and there was a drink dispenser filled with peppermint punch. Everything looked especially festive.

"I know what you should think, want to hear it?"

"No."

I turned to the room, and nodded to Mama Lucille.

She stood up from where she was knitting something and got everyone's attention. "As ya'll know, this is not quite the night you might have expected when you checked in to Snowflake Falls Inn. However, we try to be prepared for every eventuality so we can be sure you're comfortable. Tonight, our festivities will be a little different than planned, but no less fun in my opinion. The lovely Miss Hayes has prepared an evening not to be forgotten. Take it away, Molly."

"Ladies and Gentleman, the final event of the night will be a white elephant gift exchange, so your first task is to run to your rooms and choose an item, silly or serious, to wrap and swap. You'll find all kinds of wrapping on the table by the door. You have fifteen minutes to return before we start our reindeer games."

The kids went first and returned in record time. While they were gone, Lucille and I set up the stations, hoping that everyone would find them entertaining.

The rotation was simple. After being separated by the Christmas color they were wearing, red, green, and gold teams engaged in each activity. First, there was a candy cane relay where seven candy canes had to be transported from one side of the room to the other without using any hands. Next, each team got a snowman building kit, with toilet paper, for wrapping their snowman, along with hat, scarf, and paper buttons. The best snowman would win.

The next challenge was to choose one person to strap on a belt connected to a tissue box filled with jingle bells. That person had to shake their booty with enough jiggle to get all the bells out while their team cheered them on. Everyone took turns in the Christmas photo booth staged in the lobby and filled with Santa beards, antlers, Rudolph noses, and other disguises to pose with to their heart's content, while Ben willingly snapped their pictures with a modern version of the old classic Polaroid camera.

Somehow, I got roped into being on a team during the candy cane relay. It was a line up of Davenports, with Greyson strategically placed to hand his candy canes off to me. Each person held a candy cane in their mouth and used the hook to transfer another candy cane from a jar —then from person to person—to the end of the line where I would put it into a basket. The girls couldn't stop giggling. They almost fell over with their delight at seeing their parents playing like this. Vanessa kept trying to cheat by using her hands, but Jane kept her honest. Greyson enjoyed shouldering in close while attempting the hand off to me. It was impossible not to laugh when he found it essential to rub his bearded cheek against mine as he transferred the candy canes.

But that was nothing compared to the laughs elicited when Greyson strapped on the tissue box with the bells. I'd never seen anything more hilarious.

When each group had finished their rotation of festivities, they found their way back to the gathering room—with the fire roaring and candles lit everywhere—to enjoy the goodies laid out for them, and to take part in the gift exchange.

"I hope everyone's had a fun time," I said as they drifted over with plates full of reindeer game nibbles and glasses sparkling with peppermint punch. There was a generous round of approval, and it warmed my heart. "Well, good. We'll finish off the night with a good old white elephant exchange. You each have a gift and here's a bowl of instructions on whom you should trade your gift with. Now don't cheat and just go for the person with the biggest gift, because you could end up with something completely ridiculous. One year we did this with my family, and I chose a long tube hoping for … I don't know. Something long and tubular. It was a business calendar. Just what a fifteen-year-old girl dreams about."

Everyone laughed. I walked around letting everyone pick their slip from the bowl. Mrs. Davenport fluffed a hand through the papers while putting her other hand on my elbow and leaning in close. "Have you noticed anything different about Greyson?"

Willing my cheeks not to respond, I shrugged. "Did he shave?"

She giggled. "I think it has something more to do with a certain baker he can't keep his eyes off of."

A thrill of concern jolted my heart. "I'm sure—"

She stopped me by drawing out a slip of paper and unfolding it with a flourish. "I have had more fun tonight than I've had in a very long while. I may be wrong about Greyson, but I want you to know how much I appreciate your excellent efforts, Molly."

I let out a pent up breath and smiled. "Thanks, Mrs. Davenport. It's been a pleasure."

She winked and let go of my elbow so I could work my way around the room. Her comments stayed with me, warming my insides while I passed out directions. When I got to Greyson he grabbed a slip, quickly read it and tossed it back in, grabbed another and did the same.

"Hey, no choosing your slip. It's a random game, Mr. Davenport."

"I'm not choosing, I'm being selective. Ah, this will work just fine." He smirked at me and waved me on. I still could not get over how much his behavior had changed. It hurt how much I liked this funny, ridiculous, handsome, and charming young man that was hiding underneath the man I first met. It felt like Christmas. Well, of course it felt like Christmas, but he felt like a gift, even if I could only enjoy him for a few days longer. It would be a memory I would hold fondly for years to come. Never in my wildest dreams did I think I would feel that way.

Somewhere in the midst of the festivities the power did indeed go out. Ben and Lucille quickly lit the kerosene lanterns they had placed around the room as well as the candles on the mantle. In spite of my fears, the party hardly paused to recognize the change.

When the clock struck ten, everyone circled around . The kids were sleepy but enthusiastic, getting hyped up by the sugary treats. I giggled as the exchanges began, with one of the kids swapping with the person who had the fanciest ring. Vanessa Davenport won that distinction. Next, the person with the longest hair, then the person wearing the most sequins, and a person wearing black framed glasses. Lucille grinned at me from across the room. Her look said, "I knew we could pull this off."

I smiled back feeling uniquely triumphant. There was something special about creating a night when everyone was laughing, talking, and enjoying themselves without a single cell phone or social media update. Of course, it would have been an amazing boost for The Cookie Jar to be posted a thousand times on all the forums, but there would be time for that. I'd taken plenty of pictures to add to our website, and Vee would be ecstatic about all the good press when she came back. I started cleaning up, wiping away crumbs, gathering empty platters, and carrying them into the kitchen. I was exhausted after a long night and way too much emotion in the middle of my day. The party had been a much needed lift. It finally felt like Christmas.

That made me pause. I chewed on the thought that a night spent in simple revelry had done more to help me feel the Christmas spirit than a hundred fancy parties. It brought me back to those moments of my childhood when we had nothing to spend and yet we made the most cherished memories. It stemmed from the basic attitude of my mother, one that spoke of abundance when we lived on pennies, and gratitude when there was nothing to receive but everything to give. She showed me that depth of attitude made all the difference.

"Hey, you." Greyson walked into the kitchen where I was putting away the leftovers.

"What did you end up with? Toilet paper or socks?"

"So, you saw how good I looked as a toilet paper snowman?"

I turned and laughed at the memory of Greyson wrapped in tissue, a pink scarf around his neck, and a purple pompom ski cap over his head.

"You were adorable."

He ducked his head and a blush tinged his cheeks. It made me laugh harder. "Oh my goodness, is there a shy bone in your body, after all?"

"Stop it," he scolded. "Look. It says this is yours."

I looked down at the little square of instructions from the white elephant exchange. It said, "Exchange with the cutest girl in the room." I couldn't help the smile that lifted the corners of my cheeks.

"No, you're supposed to exchange with the people in the circle."

"I'm bending the rules."

"I don't have anything to swap with you."

He looked up at me quickly. "I'd take a kiss."

Cinnamon Rolls

Recipe from Jamie Burt

½ c. warm water

2 pkg. dry yeast

2 Tbsp. sugar

1 (3½ oz.) pkg. instant vanilla pudding

½ c. margarine or butter, melted

2 eggs, beaten

1 tsp. salt

8 c. flour

Filling:

½ c. margarine or butter, melted

1 c. brown sugar

1 c. white sugar

¼ c. flour

1 ½ Tbsp. cinnamon

Frosting:

8 oz. cream cheese, softened

½ c. margarine or butter, softened

1 tsp. vanilla

3 c. confectioner's sugar

About 1 Tbsp. milk (just enough to fluff frosting)

In a large bowl, combine water, sugar, and yeast. Stir until dissolved. Set aside.

In a large bowl, prepare pudding mix according to directions. Add margarine, eggs, and salt. Mix well, then add the yeast mixture. Blend. Gradually add flour and knead until smooth.

Place in a large, greased bowl. Cover and let rise until doubled. Punch down and allow to rise again. Roll dough out onto a lightly floured surface to about 34×21 inch size.

Melt butter for filling and brush on rolled dough. Mix sugars, flour, and cinnamon together and sprinkle over buttered dough. Roll dough up tightly. With a knife, put a notch along the roll every 1 to 2 inches. Use thread or a sharp knife to cut roll. Place on greased baking sheet about 1 to 2 inches apart. Cover and let rise until doubled.

Bake at 350 for 15-20 min. Remove when golden brown.

*If the rolls start to brown too quickly on the top or on the edges, cover loosely with foil to continue baking until the middle is done.

For the Frosting: Cream together cream cheese, butter and vanilla until fluffy. Add confectioner's sugar one cup at a time. Add in milk a little at a time until frosting is light and fluffy. Frost rolls while still warm.

Note: You can make the dough the night before. Prepare recipe and allow to rise once. Punch down and cover, putting in the refrigerator overnight to slowly rise. In the morning roll out dough and finish. They also freeze well once they've been baked. Warm in the microwave.

CHAPTER EIGHT

"Greyson."

I pressed back against the sink. "We're not doing this, re-member?"

"First, open it." I shook my head, but he extended the present wrapped in garish birthday paper and flashed his trademark smirk. "Scared, Cookie Girl?"

"Hardly."

"Then do it."

I narrowed my eyes at him. "This is only one of the reasons I find you absolutely annoying."

"But annoying in an adorable way, right?"

I was going to protest, but I'd already begun to pull the wrapping away to reveal a long box. Inside was a serving spoon, heavy handled with a wide swirling design. In my hand it felt comfortable and smooth. I turned it over and noticed something in the dish of the spoon. There, in uniform letters stamped into the metal, were the words "Cookie Girl."

"What is this?" I held it up to the kerosene lamp flickering overhead. "Greyson, where did you get this?"

He had ducked his head again. "I made it."

"When?"

"Please don't ask me."

"Tell me." I was too intrigued to realize I'd advanced on him with the spoon in hand, probably looking pretty dangerous.

"A week ago."

"You mean before we came up here?"

"I told you not to ask. Do you ... like it?"

"Greyson, it's ..." I didn't know what to say. It was amazing. I wanted to stamp every single utensil in my kitchen like it. Well, with "The Cookie Jar." I wasn't "Cookie Girl", after all. It was the *idea* I liked, I told myself. He couldn't be on to something about changing my business name.

"I really love it."

He looked up then, his eyes finding mine as a smile spread across his face, lifting the corners of his whiskery mouth into a perfect grin, complete with white teeth. "Cool."

And then it happened. His hands found my hips again, that grounding surface that started the fire burning through my belly and up my spine. Carefully, he edged me back against the counter in the same movement that brought him close, brushing his lips against mine.

I waited for the alarms to go off, for the feeling of protest to rise up inside of me and demand release. But it never came. Instead of resisting the fire rushing under my skin, I reached for his waist and leaned in, letting him lift me onto the counter. Long strands of my blonde hair pulled loose from the twist at my neck and cascaded over our faces as I kissed him, wrapping my knees around his waist and nudging him closer.

It shouldn't have been so easy, or comfortable, to weave my fingers into his hair and sample the taste of his lips at every angle. It shouldn't have been, but by some Christmas miracle, it was.

* * *

"There's something I need to tell you." Vee's voice on the phone was grave with an underlying hint of something else. Excitement? I held my breath. It was the first time we'd spoken since the snow set in, three days earlier. I'd spent the last half hour sharing the circus of my life with Karen. Vee was next as I snuggled in the soft four poster bed on the top floor of the inn, listening to the muted sounds of activity happening all around me while I ignored the onset of day.

I'm grateful for big fat selfish snowflakes that keep me from seeing my best friend.

"Jon proposed!"

"What? Are you kidding me? Vee! Congratulations!" I sat up in surprise, pounding on the comforter for emphasis. "Tell me everything."

"It was so romantic," Vee groaned. "I am seriously marrying the best man on the planet. I'm so sorry to snatch him up and leave everyone else in the lurch, but I can't help myself."

"You were always selfish like that," I agreed with a giggle.

"Oh my gosh. Something happened up there."

I paused, trying not to feel giddy inside. "Nothing happened."

"You are giggling, Molly Elizabeth."

"A girl can't giggle when her best friend gets engaged?" I tried to stop but it was hopeless.

"So help me, you better fess up, girl."

"I asked you first."

"Sleigh ride proposal. Now go."

"Genevieve Devereaux."

"Okay, but I am not going to be distracted, do you hear me?"

I agreed, and then listened while she described the slant of the light, the color of the horses' hair, the sound of his voice while the snow was falling, and the shape of the stone in her ring.

"I'm sending a picture right now."

"I'm surprised you didn't call the moment it happened."

"I did. You were all snowed in, or whatever. Weather can be so bratty."

"I know." I chuckled again. "Vee, I'm so happy for you."

"I am too. So happy. Jon is definitely the one. Now, I've waited long enough."

"Please don't freak out."

"I am allowed to freak out," Vee argued. I could hear her tone rising and decided to just jump in and tell her all about the kissing, the confessions, the spoon—especially the spoon—and more kissing. Vee squealed with delight so many times one would have thought this story was about her, not me. "Please tell me you loved the scruff."

"Stop. I am not going into detail."

"After all this time, you're going to leave me hanging?"

"I don't need to paint a picture." I sighed, doing my best not to giggle again. "But yes. I love it." I moaned and put a hand over my face. "I don't even know who I am anymore. Did I mention this was all your fault and how you're most definitely fired?"

"You mean, I don't have to come back for the Tenth Day of Christmas, the formal dinner, Cookie Girl?"

"Hey, you don't get to call me that." I stopped her, shaking a finger at the phone as I spoke. "He doesn't even get to call me that."

"But your spoon does?"

I sighed. She was right. I was totally losing this one. I picked up the spoon I'd set on the night stand and looked at the words pounded into the surface. "I can't do this, Vee, but I don't know how to stop. There's this un-seen force that keeps pushing our faces together."

"Nice try, Molls." Vee was full on laughing now. "You are the only person I've ever met who moans more over being kissed than *not* being kissed."

"That's because being kissed poses a problem when you've dedicated yourself to the single life. Kissing usually means you're a couple, and he's got to know that when this Twelve Days of Christmas gig is done, he won't see me again."

"For real, girl? You're hanging on to that, now?" Vee sounded alarmed. "You can't be serious."

"Vee, I've never been more serious. And he knows it. I can't do it. I can't take the risk. It just hurts too much."

I stared at the mirror but didn't see the blonde girl with flannel pajamas in it. I saw my mother reflected in the bed, her sister, Karen, sitting beside her, and the painful words echoed through my sixteen year old heart: "I could do this, Karen. I could handle it if it wasn't for her." There was a pause and then came the worst sobbing sound I'd ever heard. My mother cried over soldier re-unions, greeting card commercials, and especially poignant dances on reality TV, but I'd never before heard her sob like her heart was breaking in two. I remember wanting to pull away, to find a way to comfort myself from her pain that felt too raw for me to manage. But it was the final words that scarred my heart more than her sobs ever could.

"I wish I didn't have her."

The words stung me. They slapped me in the face and made me jerk away from the door. Those words echoed in my head as I hurried back down the hall and slid into the smallest spot possible on the couch, between my un-cle and ten-year-old Carson. They were watching a car show, and I didn't care. I couldn't see the TV through the tears blinding my eyes. I couldn't tell them why they fell silently onto my cheeks, and being guys, they didn't ask. Heck, I don't think they even noticed. But just sitting there with one arm touching Carson's shoulder, and the other nudged up against Frank's belly, made me feel safe enough to let them fall.

"Molly? Are you still there?"

"Yes, but I think you're cutting out." This time it was for real. There was a thick static chopping up her words.

"Okay, we'll be up there as soon as the roads open. Kiss that boy as many times as—" And then she was gone, and I stood there staring at the girl in the mirror for a few minutes longer.

"You know, he might be right." I told her, though she looked at me quizzically. "There might be some things that are worth the risk."

I tucked a strand of hair behind one ear and tipped my head. I wondered where he was and what he was thinking about. The night before I'd slept like the dead, missed breakfast this morning, and was now in the process of getting ready for the day. I could hear the wind howling through the canyon outside and dared to lift the heavy window coverings to check the status of our incarceration. If we'd been dreaming of a white Christmas, like Bing encouraged so many times, this was a dream come true. Glistening snow covered every surface, making the view pristine and resplendent. There was very little sun to shine on it, but what there was reflected and sparkled across the newest fallen flakes, making me wish I could go out and make a snow angel.

A sound at the door like a woodpecker tapping drew my eyes from the window. I hurried across the room, checking myself to be sure I was dressed enough for Lucille or Ben to see me.

"Was I supposed to do lunch today?" I asked, opening the door. Only, it wasn't Lucille or Ben. It was Greyson with a tray.

"Ah, Sleeping Beauty has risen."

"What's this?" A few days before, I would have made sure he never crossed the threshold, but this morning—with the tempting smell of freshly made Snowflake Falls Inn cinnamon rolls tantalizing my nose—I was only going through the pleasantries necessary to get one in my belly.

"You missed breakfast, and let's be honest, it's not something to be missed when these puppies are on the menu."

"I was tired." And I needed some yoga and Vee time. I left that out, because I wasn't sure if we were far enough along to endure downfacing dog.

"As you should be. Those parties you do are crazy, Molly. You need more help, to be honest, but first you need some cinnamon rolls, some cold milk, and a garden omelet. You like peppers, yes?"

I nodded, standing aside so he could come in before I realized I was still in my pajamas. And then I noticed he was too. Fleece bottoms with football helmets on them and a textured long sleeve waffle knit top with three buttons undone at the throat.

"You're in your pajamas."

"Not really going out much today. And it's still early … ish."

"It's almost eleven," I said.

"I threw in the 'ish.' "

"You like football?"

"Hate it."

"Okay?"

"From Vanessa. She thinks all men love football." He shrugged.

"Ah. Well, it was thoughtful."

"No, thoughtful is bringing up breakfast for your …" He paused, placing the tray on the table by the big, over-stuffed chair. "Should I call you my party planner still?"

I tried to ignore the suggestive smile on his face and the way his hair was a complete riot. He had been up nosing around the kitchen with that hair, smashed on one side with bedhead and curls askew on his forehead. It was laughable and completely sexy all at once. I chose not to notice.

"For one thing, I'm not *your* party planner. I mean, the parties are generally on your behalf because of your whole, 'I love Christmas but secretly hate it' thing, but I work for your stepmom."

"Mm-hmm, so what should I call you, Cookie Girl?"

"Not that." It wasn't as firm as I wanted it, because, darn it, Cookie Girl was actually growing on me. "Call me Molly."

"You're my Molly." He smiled, a sincere little grin that lifted on one side more than the other. "I like that."

"Not *your* Molly. Just Molly."

"But you're not just Molly. You're—"

"Stop it."

"Are you refusing to let me develop a monologue here?"

"Yes. This isn't Shakespeare. You're not Romeo, and I am definitely not Juliet. There will be no poisoning or faked deaths around here. If we're anything, we're Scrooge and Cratchit."

"You're Scrooge?" His voice was laughing and teasing all at once as he watched me pick up the fork and sort through the eggs before breaking off a piece of cinnamon roll and putting it in my mouth. There was no need to chew, the sweet bread simply melted in my mouth. My eyes drifted closed as I savored it. These cinnamon rolls really needed their own thing: their own sign on the front of the building with stars and flashing lights; a signal that lit up every time they were fresh from the oven, like a donut shop; and maybe a warning label.

"No, that's you," I said after a minute, taking a bite of eggs next.

"My grandpa loves that book. Read it to us every Christmas. I can't say I felt the same. Creepy ghosts, old men with generosity issues. I don't know."

My eyes snapped to his face as he reached over and picked up a chunk of my eggs, popping it into his mouth.

"It's a classic, Trust Fund."

"I don't have one of those, remember? You're calling me Greyson now."

"Not when you're being ridiculous about an institution of Christmas."

"Ah, I've crossed a line." He looked amused and so tempting. Gah! I needed help.

"Bolted over the line, is more like it." I put a hand on my hip. "Are you seriously telling me you don't love *A Christmas Carol*?"

"Love is too strong a word. I'm leaning toward tolerate."

My eyes narrowed. "My mother read it to me every year. It was a tradition we never missed. The story of one man's overwhelming greed transformed in one fantastic night. I think she read it to remind me that loss doesn't have to dictate our decisions. And it's never too late to change."

The words were out and I was chewing another bite before they completely registered within me. *Loss doesn't have to dictate our decisions.* The truth resounded in my chest, touching the tender parts of my heart. My head popped up, and I looked into Greyson's eyes, seeing the same light of understanding dawn there.

"Oh my gosh."

Leaving the food, I walked to the chair I'd been sitting in earlier and sank into it, my eyes drifting to the window where the world outside was painted white. Folding my legs up, I wrapped my arms around them and hugged myself for comfort. Memories of my mother were still so wrapped in the sorrow of her loss, they often felt hard to bear.

"She begged me to read it to her that year." My words were a whisper, but Greyson heard them and moved closer, leaning against the edge of the white coverlet. "I thought it was because she didn't want to miss the tradition."

The story sped through my mind on fast forward, the details jumping out at me. The grumpy miser who made his name denying others as well as himself. The haunting ghosts who warned of a misspent life. The memories of loss and sorrow that painted his life and bent his path. The change of heart that took place after seeing clearly for the first time. A tear slid down my cheek as another wave of realization hit me. I looked down at my hands clasped over my legs. "I'm Scrooge."

"What? No." Greyson moved over and crouched down in front of me. Again, I was surprised by the warmth and kindness in his eyes. "Don't say that, Cookie Girl."

"Greyson, I've lived his story. Not the money or coal part, but my heart …" I placed a hand over it. "I've been miserly with that.

"I thought it was safer to hide my love away, to avoid vulnerability and just move through life without hurting anyone. That was my goal. But I've been a Scrooge: alone, afraid, unmoved by love for a long time."

Greyson's eyes held mine. "My grandma says we deal with loss differently. I thought she was just trying to explain why I was losing it, why our family seemed to come apart at the seams when Rosie wasn't there to keep the stitches in. But she was right. For her, it's cooking. She made cookies every single day for a year. She donated them to people in the neighborhood: the mailman, the local schools. Once, she drove to another state to deliver them to the college fraternity because Grandpa was all cookied out. For her, there was something about the process of pouring sugar and measuring out dough that helped to heal her heart. Grandpa started making bird houses."

He chuckled when I lifted my brows. "I didn't even know he had the tools. Last Christmas he just came in with this birdhouse. He started selling them online. He has a business card. I'm pretty sure he's financed the college education of the guy at the hardware store with all the money he spent there."

"And you ..."

"I hide from the people I love and hate Christmas." He shook his head. "And then meet this freaking awesome girl who won't let me."

The window drew my attention again. "Your grandma has it right. Coping with cookies. She should start a foundation."

He laughed. "You two would make a good team."

I shook my head. "It's just, all this time I didn't see it. I've pushed everyone away thinking it was what my mother would have wanted. The memory of her ..."

"What?"

I shook my head pressing my lips closed. I didn't think I could say it out loud, even now.

Carefully, he took my hand and held it between both of his. "It helps to say the words, Molly. When you let me share all those things in the kitchen the other day, it felt like a burden being lifted. I want to help with your load too."

At last my eyes shifted to his, and I told him. About the tears and confession my mother made to her sister. About how it broke my heart to know she didn't want me, that even she thought being without me would have been easier. I still didn't know what I'd done to make her feel that way.

"Did you ever ask your aunt about it?"

"I have never told anyone about it until this very moment." I swiped another tear, wishing I could get my emotions under control.

Greyson touched my leg. "Molly, I think it's a misunderstanding. From everything you've told me, you were your mom's world. I don't think you heard that the way it was intended."

"That would really suck, because I've kind of built my life around those words."

"So change it," he said.

"It's not that easy, Greyson." I could feel the frustration welling up inside of me and took a deep breath.

I'm grateful for the possibility that I'm wrong.

"I know. I've walked in your shoes, Molly. I know how hard it is to lose someone and then yourself too. For crying out loud, I pretended to be a rich snob for almost a month before someone swung a Yule log at my head."

I tried not to grin, because his challenge made me furious, but the image of me smacking him with a log was too much to resist. It took the edge off my anger, and I settled back. "But where do I go from here? I want to talk with her so bad and just ask all the questions I didn't know I would need answers for. She died right when I needed her most, and it's so cruel."

"Tell me about it." Greyson settled back, leaning against the footboard of the bed. "But, to be fair to Death, there's really no good time."

"I don't think we should be concerned about Death's feelings if he's not going to be concerned for us."

Greyson grinned. "Cookie Girl, I like you a lot."

I swallowed nervously, shy with this new idea of letting someone in.

"Greyson, I don't know."

"You don't have to say anything," Greyson said in a hurry, "I just want to be sure you understand how I feel. When we met, that guy who pointed out all kinds of flaws that didn't exist, that wasn't the real me. From this point on, let's not have any confusion. This is the Greyson I want you to know. The Greyson who thinks you are the best thing I've ever seen."

"Even my Santa cookies?"

He grinned, crawling back to the chair where I was sitting and pulling me toward him.

"Especially your Santa cookies." I scooted forward, sliding my arms around his shoulders, loving the way it felt to run my fingers over the muscles there. The warm feeling in my belly returned as I looked into his eyes.

"And my chocolate popcorn?"

"Delicious."

"I don't know how to do this, Greyson," I whispered.

"I'll lead if you let me," he leaned in. "I've heard kissing is a great place to start."

"You've heard?"

He chuckled, gently gliding his nose against my cheek. "I prefer several kisses per day, as a rule." My heart was racing, and I was desperately trying not to sigh, but there was a deep feeling of relief rolling through my muscles and out through my toes. The feeling that comes after holding something tight for a long time and finally letting it go. I leaned into him, relishing the irony of his soft bearded cheek against mine and how much pleasure it brought me. I was going down hard.

"There are rules?"

"Definitely." He pulled back a little bit so I could look into his eyes. "Want to hear the rest?"

"I'm a rebel," I told him, "so rules don't apply to me."

His grin turned wicked. "I thought I was the rebel."

I shook my head. "But I will agree to one rule, Greyson."

With a lifted brow, his eyes focused in on my mouth as I spoke. I only had a few moments before I lost him entirely. "Everyday we'll be grateful."

"I'm grateful that I can't stop thinking of your lips," he said. I pressed my mouth to his and heard the soft sigh that ran through him. Wrapping my legs around his back I pulled him closer. His arms surrounded me, tugging me in tight.

My cinnamon roll wasn't as warm and soft when I finally got back to it, but it was almost as delicious as kissing Greyson Davenport.

* * *

The sun was shining two days later when Vee pulled up with Jon in tow. Her ring glinted in the sunlight when I rushed out to hug her.

"Really, you couldn't leave him for a few more days?"

"There's only five days until Christmas, Scrooge. I can't go leaving my fiancé, now can I?" She shot me a look, and I grinned at her. I'd been grinning a lot. It was totally screwing up my image. Not that I was letting it bother me—not like before. Now everyone could easily find me sneaking Greyson under the mistletoe for an excuse to take his face in my hands and press my lips to his. Long evenings by the fire found me in Greyson's lap, or right beside him until he pulled me into his lap.

"She can't live without me." Jon shrugged, his massive shoulders sliding out of his winter coat as he walked into the lobby.

"Yeah, it's been a real problem. Your one day away turned into six, Genevieve, and a ring on your finger." I was trying to scold her, but again with the grinning. She noticed.

Lifting one brow she patted Jon's arm. "I'm going to have a little talk with this girl. Baker's conference, you know."

"I can make myself at home." Jon grinned down at her, tucking her into his arms and kissing her full on the mouth before letting her go. Vee looked a little glossy eyed as she grabbed my hand and pulled me toward the kitchen.

"A little wobbly with that new ring. Is it setting you off balance?" I couldn't help but tease her.

"See, there it is again." She turned on me, her eyebrows pulled together.

"What?"

"Teasing me about Jon, and grinning."

"I always tease you about Jon." I folded my arms and tried not to smile. It was impossible.

"Mm-hmm." She shook her finger at me. "Sounds like you need to tell me something."

"I already told you."

"No, you told me about the giggling, but this smiling and teasing ... something else happened."

"If I tell you, you're not going to jump to conclusions, are you?"

Her brown eyes widened and a hand went to her hip. "I reserve the right to jump as needed. Now spill it."

It only took a few moments to tell her everything, even with the squealing. She would have loved details, about the way he kissed, our conversations in the kitchen, and everything else, but I kept her at bay.

"All I can say is, wow."

"Look who's talking, Vee. You went away for a few days and ended up engaged."

"I know." She lifted her long brown fingers and admired her ring for a moment. "I can't handle what a stud he is. I'm seriously losing it."

"Any idea when you'll make it legal?"

She shrugged. "You know, I was thinking about doing it here in the summer. Doesn't that sound lovely?"

I'd begun to have a personal affinity for Snowflake Falls Inn. A wedding here, when the grass was green and the sun was shining. That would be heavenly.

"Before we change the subject, I could use some deets by the fire tonight."

"Please, no. Cocoa, yes; girl talk, no. That hasn't changed about me, Vee. And besides, Jon is here to snuggle you by the fire."

"Oh yeah." She grinned, her face going dreamy again. "Did I mention he's a hottie?"

"Please stop saying that. I hope you enjoyed your time in the city, but I don't want to know any mushy details."

"You know you're no fun, right?"

"You picked me, not the other way around." When her right brow rose in an "oh no you didn't" scold, I hurried to add, "But I would have picked you if I was in my right mind. And I pick you now, a thousand times over."

She grinned. "Just tell me one more time how right I was."

I closed my eyes with a long suffering sigh and then admitted it. "Fine. You were right."

"I knew it! Mmm mmm! This is a Christmas miracle, I tell ya."

"Can we work on cookies, or are you going to go all Elf on me and start singing loud for all to hear?"

"Should I? Maybe I should. Girl, you don't know how many guys I've watched you reject since the day I met you. I was getting pretty worried."

"Cookies, Vee."

"Fine. But know I'm singing inside. And possibly dancing."

"Dancing is fine," I told her, spinning in a circle with a smile.

"Can I cut in?" Greyson walked into the kitchen followed closely by Jon.

"I hope we're not interrupting your catch up session." Jon was a big guy, his voice deep, his hands the size of dinner plates, but when he was with Vee there was a gentleness that came through in everything he did. It was easy to see what she loved about him, even if I did give them a hard time.

"Nope, I got everything out of her." Vee grinned at her fiancé, sliding her arms around his waist.

Greyson lifted a brow. "Everything?"

I looked up at him shyly. "I told her a little bit about our week." His smile widened bringing out the laugh lines around his eyes that I hadn't noticed at first.

"Did you tell her I'm a good kisser?"

Cranberries. I knew my cheeks were the color of cranberries. "I thought you would want to keep that between the two of us."

"Yeah, I do." He grinned, pulling me into the pantry. "Be right back, guys. We're private kissers."

In the quiet room, its walls lined with cans and baskets of food, he nudged me up against the shelves. "I wasn't sure if you would tell her."

"Neither was I, but like I said, Vee is a force of nature. Not much gets past her. And … I wanted to."

"I'm glad." He leaned down, a hand on either side of my head. "It's no secret that I think you're the most talented, loveliest, and strongest woman I've ever met."

My cheeks had just started cooling but found themselves flushed again. "Greyson, thanks. I'm sorry if I seem to be holding back. I don't want to, but it's not easy to turn off my natural tendency to hide away. "

"I hope this makes it easier," he said, lifting my chin with one finger and gently pressing his lips to mine. He moved in, sliding his arms around my back and pulling me close. Any protests I may have had were easily discarded. I was getting so much better at that. Instead of pushing him away, I was sliding my hands up his strong chest, circling his neck, and toying with the edge of his hair. While I was memorizing him, I forgot my name and the time of day. I forgot we had a formal dinner to prepare for and cookies to bake. Thank goodness I'd mixed up the dough the night before and cut out the shapes this morning, before Vee returned.

"Mmm … I … I need to make cookies." Talking against someone's lips is amazingly tempting.

"Okay, I'm going to let you go. Just … one more."

I didn't mind that his count was a little off when we stepped out of the pantry. Jon and Vee were standing in each other's arms talking. As I drew near, I could hear wedding plans, and it gave my heart a lift of hope. Maybe, just maybe, that would be me someday.

A feeling of doubt tried to nudge its way in, but I blocked it with a gratitude.

I'm grateful for pantries big enough to make-out in.

"Sorry to interrupt, but we have a bunch of fancy decorations to figure out. "

Vee kissed Jon quickly and squeezed his hand.

"We'll find a way to keep busy," Jon said. "Come on, Davenport."

Greyson winked at me on his way out the door. Vee turned to look at me with a smile that brimmed with happiness. "This day could not have started better. You said formal dinner, right?"

"Nice suits, fancy dresses, candlelight, and a full dinner. Our cook who was snowed in for the last few days arrived just before you. She's got the dinner under control. We're on dessert duty."

"I brought you a dress."

"Please tell me it's appropriate for a fine dinner and not the club."

"It's hot. That's what I'm going to tell you. And perfect. But definitely hot too."

I rolled my eyes. "So, we're doing silver everything with evergreens and cranberries splashed around."

Within the next few hours, the trays of cookies had been baked, a plan of action for décor had been implemented, and we set to work decorating the cooled trays of cookies. I slid into "the zone", decorating each cookie with graduated sizes of white and silver sprinkles and edible beads. Vee worked on the peppermint swirl cheesecake bars after turning on some music, layering and swirling as we debated color combinations for her big day.

By mid-afternoon, I was antsy and cranked up the tunes. Vee and I started to dance and giggle, shaking and twirling and doing crazy moves we hadn't pulled out since freshman year. Greyson moonwalked through the kitchen door and did a tight spin right in front of me before offering his hand. Putting my hand in his was effortless. The song was all beat and rhythm. We moved with it, twirling around the room and laughing each time a hip bumped. The feeling of energy and music mixing together revitalized every part of me. I found myself thinking gratitudes, not because I was breaking down, but because I couldn't believe how wonderful I was feeling.

I'm grateful for music that rocks me from the inside out.

I'm grateful for Greyson, and that he wants to be with me, no matter how broken I am.

The next song was much slower and we leaned back against the counter to catch our breath. Swooping my hair from my face I looked at him with a grin. "That's how I stay in shape."

"I always thought you had too nice a body to be a legit baker."

"Oh really?" He moved in close and pulled me against him, his hand taking mine, the other pressing against the small of my back so that the air between us disappeared. He moved me around the room again, this time in a waltz. It wasn't anywhere near perfect, but it felt divine. For once, it felt good to be led. I had an overwhelming desire to sigh with relief at the direction my life was taking.

"How do you do that, Cookie Girl?"

"What?"

His cheek was against mine, and I was reveling in the softness of it. "Those cookies look like a store bought ornament. How do you get such detail? I would go crazy."

"But you made that spoon, right?"

"Yeah, but knocking on a stamp with a hammer isn't so hard."

"You say that, but the intricate placement of each letter, that takes some effort, too."

"All right, I agree with that, but the level of precision you show is mind boggling. I think you need to know that people notice and appreciate it."

I leaned back and looked into his face. "Thank you. That means a lot."

"I've been watching you for a while now, Cookie Girl. You may feel that your life is better lived alone, but everyone you touch is better for it. You are meant to be more than invisible. The woman you are changes people. You need to know that."

I nodded, unable to speak. With my arms around his neck, I held him close. There was something so remarkable about the fact that only a few days before, I'd been certain my life would be lonely. And now, in the shelter of Greyson's embrace, I could see the future differently. We spun around the kitchen until I was dizzy. He held me tight when we stopped until my equilibrium returned.

"You did that on purpose."

"Hey, it's working for me." He smiled that dazzling smile that made his eyes sparkle, and I lifted up on my tiptoes to taste it.

* * *

"Where did you find this?" I was spinning around, watching the red of my skirt twirl like a ballerina.

"I have my ways," Vee said, walking out of the bathroom in a gorgeous purple gown that was cut just right for all her curves. "All I know is, Greyson is going to need to pick his eyeballs up off the floor after he sees you in that."

"And Jon will propose all over again."

"I wouldn't mind that. Nothing wrong with a little reenactment, if you ask me." Vee giggled, fluffing her dark curls and swiping some lip gloss over her full lips.

"Vee, I feel like a fairy princess."

"A Christmas princess," Vee agreed, "and those silver glitter heels take the cake. I wish I could wear them."

"The only problem with being completely different body types and shoes sizes is that we can't swap."

"Except for jewelry."

"Yes, I love these." I shook my head to make the rhine-stones in my large glitter hoop earrings shine, and I touched my throat where a single snowflake sparkled on a silver chain.

"You might not get these back, girl." Vee had silver ear-rings on too, but they were simple square cubics in three graduated sizes. Around her neck a crimson and cubic necklace glittered.

"I don't know how long I'll function in these shoes." They were three inch wedges with ankle straps. I would be almost tall enough to kiss Greyson without having to step on my tiptoes.

"Those shoes are for looking pretty in your seat, Molly. This time we're serving dessert only, so I brought these for our quick trip to the kitchen and then we can put our cute shoes back on."

She held up two pairs of fuzzy black slippers.

I looked in the mirror. My blonde hair was highlighted by a swipe of bangs that fell artfully across my face, just above one eye. The rest was twisted into curls around my head. Bold red lips. Eyes lined with just a hint of glitter at the outer edges. Red dress falling in a whirl over black glitter tights. Tonight was the only formal event we'd planned for the season. Everyone loved the chance to dress up, and no one more so than those who had money to spend on formal gowns and custom tuxes. The menu would be sublime, capped off with our special creations brought to life that morning and well into the afternoon.

Normally, I was much too worried about presentation and product quality to relax for dinner. But tonight I couldn't stop thinking about Greyson and how he would look in a suit. This delightful dinner would be our first official date.

Mrs. Davenport had pulled me aside in the hall earlier in the day, wrapping me in an awkward hug and air kissing my cheeks.

"You've worked a Christmas miracle, Molly Hayes. I don't even know who that man is, but he reminds me so much of my James now that he's remembered how to smile. The girls adore him. I know I have you to thank."

"Vanessa, I'm not sure—"

"Don't worry. Your work has been superb. I don't know how you do it all, but you have. I had every intention of inviting you to the dinner this evening, and now that I know you'll be coming with Greyson, James and I can really enjoy ourselves. This means the world to both of us, Molly."

I didn't know what to say, and thankfully Vanessa hadn't allowed me too much time to worry about it. Instead she hugged me again and then hurried off for her massage.

Now, walking to the elevator, Vee nudged me with her elbow. "I like that smile you've been wearing today. I've been waiting to see it for a very long time, Molly Hayes."

"I know." I sighed, trying not to drift off into a memory of Greyson's kiss that afternoon and the feel of his hand on the small of my back pressing me closer. "It's been so surreal. I can't believe a week and a half ago I thought he was the most annoying person on the planet. You don't think I'm being too hasty, do you?"

"Hasty?" Vee pushed the button. "If you moved any slower, I think we'd all be stuck in the dark ages. Girl, how long has it been since you kissed a boy?"

"Really kissed, or been kissed despite my protests?"

She gave me a look that showed what she meant.

"Okay, it's been … a long time." I didn't want to admit the gap in my love life. In all honesty, high school was the last time I'd been kissed by anyone I wanted to kiss in return. Most of my unwanted interchanges were a result of some blind date Vee insisted I go out on. I blamed her for my mental distress, but she took it all in stride.

"If I start to feel worried about this guy, you'll be the first to know. But let's be honest, I called it the day we met him."

"Oh please, you just thought he had a cute butt."

"And nice biceps. Girl, I picked you a good one. I intend to collect in beautiful cookies for my wedding."

"I intend to knock your socks off with my wedding cookies, but you didn't call it. You were just ogling. O.W.C, Ogling While Committed. I think you should confess to Jon."

"I wasn't ogling for me, I was helping my girl out."

I rolled my eyes, overcome by her self sacrificing. "Speaking of Jon, I need you to focus for about thirty minutes tonight. Can I count on that with him in the room wearing a tux?"

She looked at me and shrugged. "Girl, I don't know what I can handle until we give it a try. I have every intention of being present and accounted for, but if his fineness overcomes me, all bets are off."

"I will hunt down his fineness—and yours for that matter—if you don't help me prep a hundred plates. Got it?"

She saluted. "Got it. Man, having a boyfriend makes you extra sassy."

"I don't have a boyfriend," I said quickly and then clapped my hand over my mouth as the elevator doors opened. I lurched forward, jamming the closed button. I caught sight of Jon turning a quizzical look in our direction as the doors eased shut again. I pulled the stop switch.

"I have a boyfriend."

Vee took my elbows. "No hyperventilating, Molly. This is a normal process of life." Her dark eyes bore into mine. "Breathe in, Molly."

I did what she said, fanning myself, because suddenly, I was sweating like an animal that sweats. Not a dog, dogs pant. What animals sweat?

"This is normal." The words sounded muffled from the rushing in my ears. "He's great looking and good to you."

"He is good to me." I felt the swelling of tears behind my eyes and fought them back.

"You're ready for this. You've been ready for a long time. This is a good thing." Vee was petting my arm with her long elegant fingers.

I nodded, breathing deeply through my nose and letting it out through my mouth. "This is a good thing. It is."

Vee nodded, her hair bobbing as she did. "Okay?"

"Yes. I'm okay. I have a boyfriend, and it's a good thing. He's a nice guy. And a great kisser." I had to stop myself from giggling when that one came out. Holy buttercream, I was losing my mind!

"Ah, so it comes out," Vee teased.

"No. I mean he is, gah! Push the button." She did, and the elevator doors opened. Jon was now leaning against the front counter with an amused look on his face. That quickly changed to open admiration when he caught sight of Vee. My eyes scanned a room full of faces, glittering dresses, and holiday finery. Mama Lucille and Big Ben were just walking into the gathering room. Lucille was classic perfection next to a dapper Ben, but what took my breath away was Greyson Davenport passing by them. His light blue eyes were locked on me in an unmistakable look of appreciation and desire that had me tingling all the way to my toes. There was a teasing smile on his face when he reached me, noting the pink in my cheeks.

"Planning on spending your night in the elevator, Miss Hayes?"

"It's very posh in there. We could set up a table."

"Yeah, I hear that all the time." His smile widened.

"It's a thing, in nice restaurants. If you forget your tie or glass slippers, the elevator is the best you can do."

He popped out an elbow and turned with a flourish. "We've got the tie, and those shoes look way better than glass slippers. So may I escort you to your table?"

I extended my hand and let him take it, feeling the tenderness in his smile settle over me and warm me from the inside out.

"You look stunning, Molly." Greyson whispered in my ear as he guided me into the gathering room. It was transformed with tables covered in white and centered with glittering silver and white tree branches. Glitter, with white and silver candies, dusted the surface of the tables, and silver cups and ornaments brought the look together. Every place setting shone with chargers in silver, white dinner plates, and cranberry red bowls on top.

"I hope you don't mind sitting with a couple wiggly girls," Greyson said, pulling out my chair. On one side, I met the awed smiles of Emma and Jane.

"It's my pleasure," I said, turning to greet them.

"It looks like a winter wonderland in here," Jane said in hushed awe. Her dress was red velvet with furry accents that snuggled around her neck and trimmed her sleeves. Her hands we're folded in reverence to be included with the grown ups in such an event. Emma was trying ever so hard to mimic her sister's solemn posture, but she was positively wriggling in her seat with excitement.

"Can I wear your dress next year, Miss Molly? It's so perfect!" Emma was decked in gold with swirling ribbon and matching gold glitter shoes. We were the perfect compliment to each other.

I grinned. "I'll keep it in the closet for you, Emma."

She blushed with pleasure and Vanessa smiled at me. "Everything is stunning, Molly. I'm so glad you get to join us for this one." There was something special in her smile. She mouthed a *thank you* to me when Greyson wasn't looking, and I could only smile. Thanking me for enjoying Greyson's company felt like being thanked for receiving a gift.

"I think she suspects," I teased Greyson once the dishes were served.

"If she doesn't after tonight, I'm not doing my job very well."

"What job is that? I thought you were a trust fund brat."

He chuckled. "I'm never going to get away from that one, am I?"

"Tell me this, will you stop calling me Cookie Girl?"

His eyes met mine and I tried to remember what we were talking about. There was so much heat in those eyes, I wanted to fan myself. "Don't tell me you still haven't realized what an ideal title that is."

"I'm … considering it," I relented finally.

"As for my job, it's this: to convince you, with my wooing skills, that I am the only guy for you."

I tried not to choke on the Christmas punch. "Wooing skills?"

"I am an exceptional wooer." Greyson leaned in so that his lips were alluringly close to mine. "Jon can vouch for me."

"Jon, whom you've never met before today. He can vouch for your wooing skills?" He looked very much like he'd like to kiss me, but I took another sip of punch as the salads were served.

Ah, Christmas salad. Greens, mozzarella shreds, caramelized nuts, and glints of brilliant red from the tiny pomegranate arils tucked in amongst the leaves.

"I love this salad," I told him after enjoying a bite. "It's one of mine."

"You're cheating on your cookies?" Greyson looked concerned.

"Not cheating. I have a wide variety of scrumptious recipes that I intend to use in my business. I just mostly do cookies."

"I don't think you've told them that."

"The cookies are completely secure in their supremacy. It sounds like someone *else* has insecurity issues."

"I really do. I don't think I know you anymore if you start throwing around salad recipes."

"A person can't survive on cookies alone. That dinner you helped me with the other night used my recipes. One of these days, I'll cook dinner for just the two of us and you can try a few more that will utterly convince you that I am more than just cookies."

He practically beamed at me, and I couldn't understand why.

"Why are you grinning at me like that?" I finally asked as he chased down a runaway aril and smudged the tablecloth crimson.

"You said 'one of these days,' " he said, his smile still brilliant.

I shrugged. Okay, I spoke of the future. He was right. It was far outside my normal MO, but maybe I was inventing a new normal. Maybe this was my resurrection. Scrooge got his, the transformation from stubborn and stingy to a lover of all things Christmas, a man who celebrated the season throughout the year. Maybe this was my Christmas to face my trio of ghosts and find that same rebirth out of sorrow and despair and into living. For that, I was grateful.

* * *

Hot water steamed up the bathroom mirror. I used the towel from my hair to wipe a clear circle into it, eying my reflection. She sported towel dried hair that dusted her shoulder tops and sleepy blue eyes. It was the eyes that looked different. I peered closer, wondering what it was in my face that I hadn't recognized before. There were the same blonde brows, and same lashes that were barely there without mascara. There was the same nose, the same quiet little birthmark that was hidden just under the curve of my chin. Greyson had found it earlier today and kissed it, making me giggle until I could hardly breathe. No, nothing seemed different in the form or structure of the face that looked back at me, but there was an undeniable lightness. I dared to think it, dared to note: it was hope. I could see it where the corners of my mouth seemed to lift, even when I wasn't smiling, and again in the glow of my cheeks that had not been there before, even on my best days. And deep in the blue of my eyes, I could see the dissipating of shadows that had haunted me for so long.

I sighed, rubbing product into my hair. Within a few minutes, I had twisted and pinned it in sections all over my head. Tomorrow, I would have loose waves. Shimmying into my flannel bottoms, I pulled a long sleeve tee over my head and put on a pair of fluffy socks. It was almost midnight after an evening not to be forgotten. I could still feel the warmth of Greyson's arm resting around my shoulders in between courses, the way his eyes sought my face when he was talking, and the sound of laughter that filled the room as we recounted our adventures in being snowbound. Every dish was more delicious than the last. As dinner came to an end, Vee and I met up in the kitchen, carefully wrapping our fabulous dresses in aprons and then creating a dazzling plate of desserts. A square of peppermint swirl cheesecake bars, an ornament shaped cookie, and three chocolate truffles—one dusted with cocoa, one with powdered sugar, and the last one rolled in ground Reeses peanut butter cups. Placed carefully on silver trimmed dessert plates, they looked absolutely amazing. By some twist of Christmas magic, we had plated everything and sat down again, sans aprons, before the last truffle was eaten.

Greyson teased me about kicking Mrs. Claus out of her cushy job at the North Pole with all my fancy treats, Vee beamed at me from where she sat polishing off her cheesecake bar, and Mrs. Davenport kept smiling smugly in our direction. I knew that having Greyson at the table without the sass of his former self filled her with a sense of triumph. Greyson Davenport did love Christmas, as she'd supposed, and her plan to make him happy had come together in the end.

I couldn't help but smile at the thought myself.

But by this hour, with my silver dress hanging in the closet and the fire roaring in the hearth, I was ready to read myself to sleep.

The sound of the fireplace in this fanciful suite was something I'd grown to enjoy over our snowed-in season. Now, I felt myself thinking sadly of my often empty apartment back in the city. There was no fireplace or large sumptuous bed. To be honest, that apartment was more of a place marker for my stuff. When I thought of home it was not there, but at Karen and Frank's where I crashed every Friday night. Home was where my loved ones were. It was odd to think that I would be going back there soon, a changed person despite the similar features that shone in my reflection only moments before.

The bed welcomed me, propping up my book, and enveloping me into a mound of pillows. I settled in, one eye sinking closed while my body turned to putty and the world around me grew rosy. A quiet knock sounded over the crackling flames, and I tipped my head tiredly in the direction of the door, wondering if I was just hearing things. No one would need to be at my door at midnight, surely. Maybe I was already dreaming of Vee bouncing in to wake me up and trying to steal all my fluffy pillows. I let that thought drift away, my one eye sliding closed again, my body growing heavier with every passing second until I heard it again: the softest tap, three times in a row.

"I'm not home," I said just loud enough for me to hear. That noise was enough to encourage my unknown knocker.

After a long moment, where I seriously considered not ever moving again, I rolled off the bed and walked over, stifling a long yawn. Undoing the latch, I turned the handle and peered through a one inch crack into the hallway lit only by the glimmering tree lights on the landing. Though he was cast in shadow, I could tell from the height and build of the silhouette before me that it was Greyson. I took a long look, appreciating everything about the figure.

"Nice curls, Cookie Girl." His voice was low, and his whisper sounded so inviting.

"Ha ha. I thought you said no more midnight arrivals on my doorstep."

"No, I said I wouldn't drink anymore, and I won't."

"Ah, then what's this all about?"

He held up a bag of candy covered chocolates and grinned. "Just a little midnight game."

"Did you say chocolate?" I grinned at him, stepping back from the opening and letting the door swing open. He was leaning against the edge of the door jam and looked tired.

"You look like you could use a little sleep."

"I could. I'm somewhere between the junction of passing out while standing up and sleeping wherever I land."

"Then what are you doing here? Your door is five steps thataway." I pointed across the hall to the gold number 2 glinting off his door.

"But you're not in there, and two people are needed to play this game."

He walked in tossing the candies up and down. "We used to play this every Christmas. I don't think I'd want to try it with the little girls, so I hope you're game."

I wiped away a yawn. "Okay, but I can only commit if it's short. I was almost gone when you knocked."

"No worries. It's brief, but revealing."

"Hmm ... okay, come on." I grabbed a couple pillows and threw them at Greyson who caught them easily. Too easily. I grabbed another and settled in before the fire, creating a pleasant pile of fluffiness to lean back against while stretching my toes toward its warmth.

"Comfy?" Greyson was grinning at me.

"These pillows," I sighed, "are the most comfortable things, ever. I might try and sneak them home."

"Most people take the complimentary soaps."

"Oh, I'm taking those too. But the pillows ... they'll never miss them."

"And you'll raise no suspicion carting out a half dozen of them."

"Exactly." I grinned at him and then I remembered my lack of makeup and my pin-curled hair and blushed. "You could have come by before I washed my face, you know?"

"I like you without makeup. I didn't know you had those cute little freckles on your nose."

"Oh, those." I touched the bridge of my nose thoughtfully. "Yeah, I guess they get hidden most of the time. What game are we playing with all this chocolate?"

"Well, you might think it sounds silly, but it's really kind of awesome. It's a color and question game. Every year our answers would change and it gave us a chance to get to know one another again. I think my grandma started it to try and figure out what to get us for Christmas."

"A color and question game, huh?"

"Right. You choose a candy in each color and then you eat the rest while you're talking." He handed me a rainbow of colors and then placed another handful on the pillow beside me. I popped one into my mouth and let it melt on my tongue while I waited. "Choose a color."

"Blue." I held it up for him to see. It may have just been me, but he was sitting very close, and the comfort of his presence was sinking into the marrow of my bones,

222 · CHRISTENE HOUSTON

warming me up from the inside out and making my nerves sing with anticipation.

"Favorite color?" he asked.

"Hmm?" I'll admit I was already distracted, thinking about the way his lips curved so nicely when I kissed them. "Oh, color. Yes. I like robin's egg blue, though I have to be honest, my color preferences range far and wide. This week it's blue and next week it could be gray. "

"I like blue too, but perhaps my color and I are in a more stable relationship."

"You just like plain blue?"

"No, I like 'Molly's eyes' blue. We can submit it to the crayon company for their new color."

I blushed, shy to look into his eyes again after that comment. "Stop it. You can't base your favorites on my features."

"Then, no 'Molly's sexy legs' as my favorite thing to stare at while eating cinnamon rolls?"

I pulled my legs up. "No!"

"Great. Next you'll tell me no 'dreaming of Molly's lips' as my favorite daydream." He pouted.

"Stop it." I was laughing too hard to really give that command the weight it needed. "Get to the next question."

"The next one. Oh yeah. Okay. Here it is, ready?"

"Mm-hmm." I stretched my legs back out and waited.

"Share something you learned last week."

"Oh …" I looked up at the ceiling as the week ran through my mind in a flash, highlights popping up like popcorn kernels. "Okay. I don't mind being snowed in except for the shower schedule. That made me feel like I'd joined the army. Five minutes is not enough for this girl."

"What? That's what you got from last week?" He looked exasperated.

"Did you learn something else, Greyson Davenport? Maybe you should share your own experiences instead of dissing mine."

"Fine, I will. I learned that I love the sound of your laugh," here he held up his hand because I was starting to protest that he couldn't keep bringing me into the conversation, "*and* I learned that I'm not very good at finding the perfect Christmas tree."

I laughed again and then blushed, remembering our Christmas tree expedition and how that had ended. "I never did get my tree."

"Yes, but now you live on the third floor where a beautiful tree is only steps from your door."

"But I still can't fall asleep under it," I mourned.

"Oh, yeah. That could be awkward—and possibly dangerous with that train chugging around it night and day." Greyson shook his head. "Okay, my turn. I pick orange. Share something you do well."

"That's easy. Cookies."

"Something I don't already know."

"That's not fair. You know I dance, too."

"Dig deep, Cookie Girl."

I tapped my finger to my lips trying to come up with some hidden gem to share with him. "Oh! Ice skating. I can skate backward and do twirling thingies and the occasional leap, even. I'm a fabulous skater. If I hadn't settled on cookies I might have been an Olympic figure skater."

"Wow, I never knew. You didn't skate when we were at the rink."

"Because I was busy serving cocoa and hand-cut marshmallows, and glaring at you."

"I felt it. I think you burned a hole in the ice."

"Serves you right."

"I can sing."

I stopped and sat up straight. "You can what?"

"Sing. Like an angel."

"Stop, really?"

"Grandma says so. And sometimes … when Rosie was having a tough night, she would ask me to sing to her."

I touched his knee, slipping my hand into his. "Greyson, that's so tender. Sing for me."

I expected him to balk and try to get out of it, but he just settled back, pulling me into his lap and settling my head against his chest. It was a unique place to be while he filled his lungs and sang to me. The world wrapped itself in velvet while he sang and when he was done, I couldn't stop smiling.

"What's your favorite Christmas carol?" he asked when he'd finished.

"You're not going to like it."

"Why?"

"It's not 'Rudolph' or 'Silver Bells'."

"For shame," he teased, squeezing me tight against him for a moment. "What is it?"

"It Came Upon A Midnight Clear."

"Hmm. Why?"

"I just remember my mom singing it to me when I was little. She would tuck me in under the Christmas tree and stroke my hair while she sang it and she would cry …always. She loved the music of Christmas. She would say if we listened hard enough, maybe we would hear the angels sing too. I never heard them, Greyson, but I swear when she sang that song, I felt this burning in my heart like maybe she was the angel, after all."

He held me close and though I felt silly telling him that at first, by the time I was done I didn't anymore. Instead, I felt warm and safe and heard, and because it was

something I had not felt in so long, I felt a surge of emotion that had tears pressing themselves against my eyes.
But then he started to sing again. The sound rose from
his chest and surrounded us in my little room with the
fire going. The power of that carol enveloped us and
deepened the feeling, sinking us into it, burying us under
a blanket of peace and stillness.

"Your turn," he said after a long quiet moment when I
was almost asleep.

I extended my arm to reach for another candy, but
they were too far away and I didn't have the will to pull
myself from his arms.

"I pick brown," I murmured.

"Something you can't live without."

"You first." I was losing the battle quickly, my eyes
sinking closed and then fluttering open again. I could feel
his breathing deepen as he answered.

"Molly Hayes. I can't live without you."

I smiled. He was so sweet when he was sleepy. "You
won't have to."

* * *

The phone rang somewhere in the darkness of a very
early morning. I was on the floor, but not cold. There
was something amazingly warm and cozy I was snuggled
up against. Oh my goodness, it was Greyson! I shot to a

sitting position and touched my hair. In pin curls. My brain flash danced through the night before, and I sighed, grateful nothing crazy had happened. We hadn't even kissed. Hmm … maybe I should do something about that.

My phone started ringing again, and I stumbled as I stood up, trying not to kick anything important. The fire in the grate was very low, and stepping out of the circle of Greyson's arms was like stepping into a snow bank. I shivered, grabbing the gold throw from the bed to wrap around my shoulders as I opened the drawer where my phone was charging.

"Hello?"

"Molly! Thank goodness. We've been calling for the last hour."

"Carson? I'm sorry. I went to bed late. I must have been sleeping too soundly. What's wrong?" There was a sinking in my chest, a solemn, horrible feeling that started at the sound in his voice and leapt to life with every syllable he spoke.

"It's Dad."

Peppermint Swirl Cheesecake Bars

Recipe from Janeen Donat

Crust:

    2 c. finely crushed chocolate wafer cookies

    2 Tbsp. sugar

    1/3 c. butter, melted

Cheesecake:

    2 8oz pkg cream cheese, softened

    1 c. sugar

    1 tsp vanilla

    1/4 c. milk

    5 slightly beaten eggs

    1/2 tsp peppermint extract

    red food coloring

    1/2 c. crushed peppermint candy canes

Preheat oven to 350 degrees F. Grease the bottom of a 9x13 in. pan, set aside.

For crust: in a medium bowl, combine crushed cookies, 2 T sugar, and the melted butter; stir until coated. Press mixture evenly into bottom of prepared pan. Bake in preheated oven for 10 mins.

For filling: in a large mixing bowl beat cream cheese, 1 c. sugar, and the vanilla with an electric mixer on medium speed until smooth. Beat in milk until combined. Stir in eggs.

Transfer 1 c. of the cream cheese mixture to a small bowl; stir in peppermint extract and enough red food coloring to make desired color. Pour the plain cream cheese mixture over partially baked crust, spreading evenly. Drizzle red cream cheese mixture over plain cream cheese mixture. Use a thin metal spatula to gently swirl the mixtures.

Bake in the preheated oven for 20 minutes, or until set. Cool in pan on wire rack for 1 hour. Cover and chill for 4-24 hours. Cut into bars. Sprinkle bars with crushed candies before serving. Makes 32 bars.

CHAPTER NINE

A sob caught in Carson's throat and my heart stopped beating.

"Carson, what's wrong?" I heard Greyson sit up, and I turned away from him to hide the terror creeping over my skin.

"He fell today. I thought maybe he was just joking around, but Mom called an ambulance. He had a heart attack, and they're taking him in for emergency bypass surgery sometime in the next hour."

"Carson, will he be okay?"

"I don't know, Molly. Mom's at the hospital, and I'm here at home with Hannah, but I can't stand it. I need to be there with them." I could hear him crying, and in my mind I was back at the hospital hearing them tell me that my mom was dying. That she only had hours to live. That the cancer we thought we had beaten was taking her away.

I shook my head trying to think of something to be grateful for, but I couldn't form the words.

"Carson, take Hannah and go. I'll meet you there."

"Mom said to stay here—" Carson started.

"I know she did, honey, but she needs you. She's being the mom and trying to protect you, but no one should be standing in the hospital alone right now. I'm on my way." I felt the words coming out of my mouth but didn't know who was speaking them.

"Okay. Thanks, Molly. I'm really freaked out."

"Don't worry, bud. I hope everything will be fine. You know your dad's a fighter." My voice sounded hollow and my hands shook. It felt like I was repeating what everyone wanted to hear and what had been said about my mom a hundred times over. The darkness in my stomach doubled and roiled, and I felt like I might be sick. Hanging up the phone, I leaned heavily on the bed, squeezing my eyes shut.

I'm grateful … I'm grateful …

Nothing came and the darkness unfurled its wings, filling my chest. I hurried to grab my keys, hat, and coat, pulling my boots on as I went.

"Molly, what is it?"

I started, surprised to see Greyson standing in my room. Something about his face registered but not deep enough to make sense.

"My uncle had a heart attack. I need to go."

"I'll get my keys."

I stopped, turning to him. "No. Greyson, don't. I can't ask you to leave your family so close to Christmas."

I'm grateful ...

It was like a motor that couldn't start, revving over and over again only to fade away. The darkness inside became a black hole sucking up all the light that was glimmering there only moments before. Frank could be dying. Frank who had been like a father to me, who had taken me on my first date, who made the most amazing Saturday waffles, and who let me cry on his tie at my mother's funeral. Frank, whom I allowed myself to love.

"You're not asking. I want to, Molly."

"Please, don't." I couldn't raise my voice, couldn't do more than gasp for air. I turned away from him, unable to watch the hurt look in his eyes. "I need to do this alone."

"But you don't have to. I know you're worried. Let me be there for you."

"No!" Finally the word came out with force. Panic was filling me, the darkness seeping into every vein and cavity. All I could see was an ending. A cosmic answer to the hope I saw in my reflection the night before, a reminder that everything good, everything beautiful, ends. Not when I'm ready for it, not when I've said my goodbyes.

No, loss perches, waiting for the right moment to crush you to the earth and steal away your tomorrows. Letting Greyson in was such a mistake.

"What did you say?" Greyson looked pale.

"This was a mistake, Greyson. I'm sorry. I should never have done this." I pushed past him and out the door.

Outside, the night was bright from the full moon gazing at its partial reflection in the snow. It was an aching reminder of the same bright reflection only a week before when I found Greyson on my doorstep. I knew, then, that I was softening, easing away from the fears of my past and opening my heart to something more. It was a horrible mistake. Life was reminding me of that. Life, with its heavy handed pain, was holding me under water, asking if I really wanted to breathe. I let the tears fall as I drove, letting Greyson go, feeling the swell of regret that filled the space in my heart even as I realized that letting go now was a gift. To him and to me. I didn't know how I could do the same with Frank. I prayed I wouldn't have to.

The hour drive to the city felt like days. Every moment that ticked by was an I-told-you-so reminder that love can overcome many things, but death isn't one of them.

* * *

"Christmas in the hospital." Frank's croaking voice woke me up with a start. I was half slumped in a chair next to a cup of cold hospital cocoa.

"Good morning, Frank ... I mean, good night. I don't even know what time it is," I said with half a laugh as tears filled my eyes. He looked worn down and pale. Aunt Karen would be irate at her well-timed bathroom break. We'd spent a day waiting through his surgery and long hours in the cardiac ICU. Half of today was more of the same. Then we waited for the removal of his tubes so we could come in and visit. When we were finally admitted, he was in a deep sleep so we waited some more.

"What's this?" His voice was tired and rough after having a tube down his throat. "You thought I was a goner, didn't you?"

I shook my head. "Of course not. I was just ... worried."

"You should have known I wouldn't take off during the holidays. I just overdid it."

"I think you should know one of your arteries was 95% clogged. You're so busted."

Frank half-grinned, his eyes drooping closed. "Karen's going to have my head for all those bratwursts I've been sneaking."

"She's going to kick your butt, Uncle Frank."

"You're still crying."

"I know." I swiped a hand under my nose. It was disgusting. "I can't help it. I was just … I was really shocked. I drove down right away."

"I hear you've got a boyfriend," he said, though his eyes were drifting shut again. "I was starting to worry."

"You were worrying about me?" I laughed. "Don't worry about me. I'm fine."

"No." His eyes opened for a long moment. "You're not fine. You're alone. There is nothing fine about that, Molly."

"I'm fine alone, Frank."

He shook his head firmly, his eyes closing again. "There is no one on this planet who can really live life without the love of another human being. I know that. I thought I was fine before Karen, but I would give up brats forever if it made her happy now. Do you understand me? Don't go repeating that, either. I kind of like a brat now and then."

I smiled, wiping away more tears. "I won't."

"Don't give up on this process, kid. During my thrilling ambulance ride, ya wanna know what I was thinking about? My kids. My wife. And how she would kick my tail if I left her at Christmas."

"She would," I agreed.

"Yes, I would, you big jerk. You scared the crap out of me. And 95% clogged? What the heck have you been eating?" It was Karen, her smile wider than I'd ever seen it, her eyes full of tears as she broke in, rushing to take his hand. He had at least a week of recovery before we could bring him home. I was sure Karen would find a way to make the holiday in the hospital just as special as it would be at home.

I chose to go for tissue before I had to resort to using my T-shirt. Carson and Hannah passed me in the hall, exchanging hugs before washing up to go into their dad's room. I blew my nose and tried to breathe deep.

I'm grateful …

Closing my eyes, I tried it again, expanding my lungs, exhaling slowly, searching for light.

I'm grateful for amazing surgeons who saved Uncle Frank.

The tears came again as my heart filled. I was happy to be grateful again. With keys in hand, I drove to their house and crawled onto the couch. Guppy's head popped up from his bed nearby looking forlorn and worried.

"You too, Gup? Come on up here, buddy." He joined me without any further encouragement, resting his head on my arm as I buried my face in his fur, and cried.

* * *

Guppy didn't move from my side the whole night. After crying myself to sleep, I woke restlessly throughout the night to find his comforting form nearby, warming me up when I felt as cold as ice. Around two, I gave up trying to sleep and went to the kitchen, washing my Guppy hands, and pulling my hair into a twist at the back of my head. Rummaging through the pantry, I gathered cream cheese frosting, devil's food cake mix, and some peppermint candies, taking them to the kitchen. This little kitchen was nothing like the one at the Davenport's or the industrial one at the inn. It was cozy, had outdated appliances, and was short on counter space. I took out a wooden spoon and mixed the cake mix with an egg and some oil until it was a thick dough. In a pot on the stove, I broke off some pieces of a chocolate bar and mixed in a mug of milk, scalding it before adding some cocoa and powdered sugar. When that was well mixed, I tipped it into my favorite mug. I stirred and sipped while turning on the oven. At the sound of it heating up, Guppy's head popped up to the top of the couch. He eyed me carefully, well versed in the fact that me plus the oven meant tasty scraps.

Pulling out a pair if cookie sheets, I worked the cake dough into small, uniform balls, letting my mind wander. Where it went was predictable, at this point. I could still feel the imprint on my hip where Greyson's hand had rested when we both fell asleep. That spot seemed to heat up at the thought, and I shivered, remembering the silkiness of his voice over my favorite Christmas carol. What a surprise he had been. At first, I could hardly stand to see the man walk in the room. Though, to be honest, I'd always admired his biceps and strong back.

Once the pans were dotted with cake-mix cookie balls, I slipped them into the oven. I leaned against the counter while they cooked and tried not to feel completely lost. My thoughts wandered from Greyson to Frank and his words when he'd come to. I couldn't argue with his point of view, but to be honest, I'd never felt more confused. I could still remember the feeling of darkness unfurling in my chest, capturing my mind in its heartless grasp. In that moment, I thought nothing in the world could ever be right again. Was it fair to put Greyson through that, knowing how easy it was for me to slip away from him?

I was interrupted by the beeping of the oven and then the opening of the door as Karen and snow rushed in. She looked up from shaking out her coat and hanging it on a peg.

"Rough night?"

I nodded, sliding in another pan and picking up my mug.

"Your mother used to cook, too, when she was troubled by something."

"Yeah, I think I learned it from her."

She lifted the tub of frosting. "Homemade Oreos?"

"A Christmas tradition." I shrugged. "Didn't think you and the kids should miss out."

She walked around the kitchen when my voice broke and wrapped me in her arms, her sniffling joining mine.

"Don't worry now, Molly dear. He's going to be fine. That big, stubborn man. He's sore and grumpy, but he's going to be just fine." A tear dripped onto my cheek from hers, mingling ours together until she looked down and gently used her fingers to wipe my face. "He owes me big time next year."

"He sure does. I mean, what kind of gift do you give someone after trying to scare them to death?"

"I think that's a diamond infraction, don't you?" Karen chuckled, swiping her dark hair from her eyes and taking the oven mitt from me. The timer had beeped and she pulled out the other pan of cookies.

"At least diamond. You can up the carat size with how long it takes him to get back on his feet and make us waffles for breakfast."

She grinned. "You know, that was one of the first things I thought about. How my life would be so different without his waffles. I think we take people for granted, no matter how we try to cherish them. I hope I've learned my lesson."

This time I hugged her, and we just held on for a long moment, letting the air filled with the scent of cooling cookies wrap around us.

"I'm sorry you had to come rushing down, Molly. I know you left someone important on the mountain."

I shrugged. "Vee can handle things. I'm sure she'll do a fabulous job. I can go and help her pack up in a few days."

"I'm not talking about Vee, or your job with the Davenports, honey. I was talking about one person specifically."

I avoided her gaze. "There's nothing really happening there, Karen."

"That's not how it sounded when we talked last week." Karen tipped her head to see my face better. "Unless something happened?"

I shrugged again. She sighed, twining an arm around my waist and leading me back to the couch. Guppy flopped down and hurried to look for cookie crumbs in the kitchen. We settled into the sofa, leaning back against the cushions. "Tell me what happened."

"It's nothing. He's just not my type. I was rushing into things, forgetting ..."

"Forgetting what, Molly?" She waited for a long moment while I fought with the words in my throat and the emotions bubbling up inside me. Having already allowed the dam to break only made it harder to hold back the flood when I spoke.

"I forgot that I'm better off alone."

"Why would you say that?"

"I can't do this," I told her. "I thought my heart would explode when I heard about Uncle Frank. I was filled with dread like I haven't felt in …"

"Six years."

I nodded, tears streaming down my cheeks and falling onto my shirt.

"I thought this young man of yours would have come with you. I'm surprised, frankly." Karen was still watching me.

"I … I told him to stay. I told him it was a bad idea … the two of us."

"Molly," Karen turned so she could see me better, taking both my hands in hers, "why did you do that?"

"When Mom died, I didn't know if I would ever find the light again, Karen. I was so depressed and heartbroken. I heard her tell you she wished I wasn't around."

Karen's eyes widened in surprise. "What? When?"

"That day after the doctor gave her two weeks."

Karen looked puzzled, and then a dawning came over her face. "You overhead us when we were talking in the bedroom." I nodded, starting to hiccup.

"She would never have told me to my face, but I know how she felt. I've known all this time. She wished she never had me. I made it harder on her. I tried so hard not to, but I did."

"Now you listen to me, young lady," Karen gripped my hands hard, "your mother loved you more than life itself. More than *life* itself, do you hear me? What she said when we were talking was that she could let go if she didn't have you. She was in so much pain, Molly. Her body was giving out on her. But she had to fight because she had you, and she needed you to know that she gave her all to stay with you. That's what she was talking about. She wished she didn't have to leave you alone. If she didn't have you, she could go without regret, but there would never be a day she missed that she would not long to spend it with you. You were her life, sweetheart."

I looked up at her bright blue eyes through my tears. "I loved her, too, and when I thought she didn't want me, it broke my heart."

Karen closed her eyes and let out a sigh filled with sorrow before pulling me close. "You poor thing. I thought you knew how she felt about you. Watching the two of you, there was no question."

"I did know. I thought I knew. But cancer … it changed things. What I thought I knew, what I thought I hoped … it all faded away into gray when I couldn't help her. I was still so young and foolish. Sometimes, I just had my priorities all mixed up. When I heard that, I guess it confirmed what I feared in my own heart: that I was a burden to her."

"It makes more sense why you hurt for so long when she passed. We hurt, too, but you just fought it so hard. You just disappeared for a long time. The girl we knew faded. It wasn't until you started talking again that we had hope you would find this girl again, this girl who is funny, intelligent, and full of life."

The realization that Greyson was right shook me. Hearing the words, and aligning them with what I had believed about myself for so long, took a moment to reconcile.

"You know, I was going through a file looking for important papers while Frank was in surgery. I found something. I didn't realize your mom hadn't given it to you earlier. It was my understanding that she left it in one of your cookbooks, but maybe she didn't get the chance. I think it's something you need to see."

"What is it?"

Karen smiled at me and stood up, walking into her bedroom and returning with an envelope.

"A letter."

I looked at her in shock. "From my mom?"

"From your mother."

I pulled my knees up, hugging myself as I looked at my name in her still familiar script. "For me?"

"You were her one and only, sweet girl. Why don't you look at it while I get washed up."

I stared at it for a long time, listening while the shower started in the back room, and watching Guppy from the corner of my eye as he slunk over to his bed by the fire. He placed his head on his paws and looked at me as if to say he was only a few steps away if I needed him.

It was a long moment before I could slide my finger under the flap to break the seal and slip the page from its cover. I opened it carefully, hit by the vague fragrance of her body lotion all these years later. The scent alone took me back in time to that last night when we laid together, reading *A Christmas Carol* in the summertime because she didn't want to miss anything.

Tears filled my eyes, but with a few tissues in hand, I unfolded the pages.

Holiday Homemade Oreo Cookies

Recipe from Janeen Donat

> 1 egg
> 1/2 c. vegetable oil
> 1 devil's food cake mix
> 1 container of cream cheese frosting
> crushed peppermint candies

Whisk the egg with the oil, then add the cake mix and mix until well combined.

Roll into uniform balls and place on a parchment paper lined cookie sheet.

Bake at 350 degrees F for 10 mins. Let cool on sheet for 1 min then move to wire rack to finish cooling.

When cookies are cool, frost the bottom of a cookie with the cream cheese frosting, roll the edges in crushed peppermint and then top with another cookie to make a sandwich.

Chapter Ten

The date at the head of the letter told me why it didn't make its way into my cookbook. It was written just a few days before she died. By then, she was pretty weak. It showed in the slant of her pen and the shakiness of the letters.

My Dearest Molly,

It's unfair. This whole cancer thing. When I get to the other side, I intend to file a complaint, and I'll just sign your name to the petition for good measure because I know you agree.

Today they told me it was the end of the road. The enemy has fanned out throughout my body and this skin that has held me together is no longer feeling up to the task. I look in the mirror and see wrinkles and laugh lines, and I love every little bit of it. I cherish it and thank my body for all it has done for me. It would be easy then, to say goodbye in reverence for all that I have been given. Except for you.

Except for the perfect gift of a daughter that you are. Except for your smile. Your energy and intelligence. Your every breath makes me hate cancer and regret the journey of death with a vengeance. It's not the path I want. I want to hold you in my arms and read about Scrooge and his ridiculous outlook on life and how it changed in one miraculous night. I want to see you walk to your diploma in High School, in College. I want to gather your gorgeous blonde curls under a veil on your wedding day and cry on the front row. I want to hold the perfect little babies you will make, who will look just like you: all golden hair and blue eyes. I want to breathe a little longer the same air that you breathe, my beautiful, intelligent, magnificent daughter.

I will regret missing every single moment. If I have any pull, I promise to watch over you. And even if I don't, I will move heaven and earth to make it happen. Of that you can be sure, my darling girl. Because there will never be a place on this earth, or any other, that is complete without me and you together.

Now, enough about me.

This letter is for you, Molly. I need you to know that you are strong enough for this. It's going to hurt. I'm so sorry I won't be here to hold you and dry your tears. But, you won't be alone. I want you to remember that.

When you go to college and you start your little bakery, I want you to make something amazing and name it after me. Promise me it will be chocolate. With nuts. And maybe a shortbread crust. Ha ha!

I have a feeling this will be one of the toughest challenges that you will face. I see it in your face, honey. I know you think that you can't make it without me. That's not true. You are stronger than you know. Being alone will be hard, but you can handle this. Just don't go too far the other way. When you've pulled yourself out of that darkness that is mourning, don't forget that loving people is the only reason for living this life to begin with. Do you hear me, Molly dear? It will be scary to love someone the way we have loved one another. To love with your whole heart, without holding back, with your arms wide open. You've loved me like that, and can I tell you what an honor it has been to live in the shelter of that kind of love? It has made cancer bearable. It has made my life worth every single breath. Loving like that will feel like you're setting yourself up for pain and heartbreak. And maybe you are. But I want you to know something. My life would be nothing, a complete and total waste, without the people I love. Without you. Without Karen and her family. Without that crazy puppy, Guppy. Man, can that boy slobber!

You may think it will be easier to avoid the pain and uncertainty that can come with loving someone. I can attest that there is nothing easy or comfortable about opening your heart to someone else. It's dangerous and daring. It's terrifying and electric. It is living with a capital L. I know because I have loved you and that is when my life became my LIFE.

So, my dying wish (See what I did there? Now you HAVE to honor it. You do what you have to when you're a mom, you'll see), my dying wish is for you to be brave and passionate and loving, and to share your life with someone else no matter how frightening the prospect.

My dearest Molly, let someone love you, and be courageous enough to love them in return. And when you do, don't hold back. Scrooge had it right. When he saw the light of his wasted, miserable, lonely life, he had it right. He was a changed man from that moment on, and he lived Life as it should be lived. When you get that chance, sweet girl, I hope you will take it like he did, with both hands so that others will say that you knew how to live Life well, if anyone alive possessed the knowledge. That's what I al-

ways loved about Christmas. Knowing that one person's love can change the world.

Don't forget, I'm watching and taking notes for when we get together again, because if I have my say, I will never be far away.

All my love, my darling girl,
Your Loralai – Mom.

To say I sobbed through the letter would be an understatement. Just seeing her handwriting was enough to put me over the edge after the night I'd been through. To read her words took me back to that day when she took her last breath and broke an unspoken promise to never leave me alone. I could hear her saying the words in my head, feel the inflection of her beautiful voice. I longed for the touch of her arms around my shoulders and the sound of her laughter ringing in my ears, warming my heart and giving me courage.

Courage to love someone else. It felt too terrifying, and like a revelation at the same time. How could she know that this letter, stained and smudged with her tears, would be found today, a few days before the Christmas I fell in love.

I gasped. I fell in love. Holy buttercream. I. Fell. In. Love.

And somehow she knew. The thought wrapped me in a homemade biscuit and melted butter over my head. It was a feeling of warmth and peace and perfect connection to someone who could no longer be in my life every day and yet somehow could. I didn't see a ghost or a shining light, but I felt the presence and love of someone who promised me she would always be near.

* * *

It was very early the day before Christmas when I pulled away from the house. After making Karen and the kids a delicious dinner—and finishing off the homemade Oreos by sandwiching cream cheese frosting between two cookies and rolling the edges in crushed up peppermint candies—I thanked Guppy for our snuggle by feeding him some homemade doggie treats I'd prepped for the season, and hugged everyone goodbye. They promised to give my love to Frank, as he continued to recover in the hospital.

Knowing Frank was in good hands gave me courage to leave the family and make things right. Hannah was the only one with an I-told-you-so look on her face. It seems teenagers have an especially long memory when they call your disgust for the rich guy passion in disguise. I may have shoved an Oreo in her face.

The sun was shining, though it was feeble. It would not do much to the snow piled up on the roadsides, but I still felt it might be a good omen.

I'm grateful for sunshine on a snowy winter day.

I'm grateful for the satisfaction of smashing an Oreo into Hannah's smug mug.

Maybe I could do this terrifying thing, and it would be okay. Maybe Mom was right. Loving someone was Living with a capital L and all this time I'd just been making do. Maybe if I went back, Greyson Davenport—rich, troubled, gorgeous, and scruffy—wouldn't laugh in my face and run in the opposite direction. Because, honestly, as messed up as I was, he had every right to.

Christmas music sang to me all the way there, chasing out my fears until the last mile when they began gnawing like termites at my stomach. I almost threw up once, and the rest of the time I was perpetually queasy awaiting the turn in the road when the inn would come into view: the white trim popping out from the red paint, the roof smothered in snow, and the walk freshly shoveled. Or it should have been. People were seriously falling down on the job lately.

I parked and tromped to the small cabin. Vee was blowing up my phone during the entire drive. It only ramped up my feelings of anxiety. At the door, I knocked, waiting for it to swing open and reveal Vee in all her fluffy curls and sharp brown eyes, seeing through my overly bright smile to the tears that threatened to spill down my cheeks.

Instead of Vee, it was Jon. I took a step back from the door because he always just seemed so flippin' tall to me. "Hi, Jon. Is Vee around, or is she too busy texting me to actually talk?"

He chuckled, that big rumbling laugh of his that came from somewhere in his massive chest. "Nah, she's just making some hot cider. Calms her down when she's all riled up."

"Riled up because she's happy to see me?"

He lifted an eyebrow. "There's no one she likes seeing better, but I think there's a bit more to it." He stepped aside and let me slink in like a bad puppy, walking to the fireplace to return the feeling to my fingertips while dishes rattled in the kitchen.

"How bad is it?"

"Are we scaling things now?" There was that chuckle again. Something about it took the edge off my nerves and brought my shoulders down from around my ears where I'd hunched them up.

"I've made a mess of things," I sighed, looking into the flames and wishing this day was over already. I was ready for tomorrow when all the I'm sorries had been said, and I knew for sure that I could get back what I'd left behind.

Right now, in front of the fire, there were no guarantees. Not everyone gets second chances.

"You're darn right you did." Vee's voice behind me made me turn. Tears were on my cheeks before she could say another word, and it made her sigh. "Come here."

Jon had disappeared, which seemed incredible for someone so large. I walked to her, sniffling, and she took me into her arms. "What the heck, girl? A text that your uncle is in the hospital, and that's it? You think that's enough?"

I shook my head against her shoulder, sorry for the tears I was leaving on her red cashmere. "I'm sorry. I was in a panic."

She hugged me tighter. "So was I. You're not a flight risk most of the time. You always talk to me, and when you didn't, I was afraid."

I pulled back, hugging myself as I said the words. "It wasn't just Frank. It was Greyson too. I ended things with him in a terrible way."

She nodded. "I know."

"What?"

"He was here after you left, trying to figure out what to do." She spoke softly, and I knew there was bad news attached to that voice.

"I told him it was a mistake." Whispered words so they didn't sound so horrible, so cutting. They hurt coming out this time.

"He was pretty upset, Molly." More tears, miserable and hot. I'd finally figured out that I didn't want to be alone, but was it too late?

"I was terrified when they called about Frank," I said between gasps. "I thought he was going to die, and it was this great cosmic witness that I should never have let Greyson in. All I could think that whole drive was that everything I love gets taken away. There was this darkness in my chest I thought would drown me. I was a mess, Vee."

"Shh." Vee took me to the couch, sinking onto the cushion and stroking my hair.

"You don't have to explain it to me, girl. I know you through and through, and I love you anyway. Do you understand that? Is that sinking into your thick skull? I love you like a sister because you are a valuable person in my life. With the darkness and the laughter. I know them both. I would not be the fabulous girl I am today without you. Do you get that? You are important to people, and they are important to you whether you admit it or not."

256 · CHRISTENE HOUSTON

I was nodding. "I get it. I've just been so afraid. My mom left me this letter, and ... I talked to Karen. I just want to make it better, but I'm afraid it's too late."

"Too late is when they lay you in the ground, Molly. While you are breathing, too late doesn't count. You make amends. You fight for what you love. You do it while you're still breathing whether the outcome is what you hoped for or not. Because it's not about you getting what you want, it's about following your heart and being willing to let the cookie crumble as it will."

"Nice cookie metaphor."

"You know it." Vee grinned at me, but there was still sadness in her eyes.

"I'm sorry I pushed you away. You've been a better friend than Lane was to Rory."

"Was Lane the Asian girl with the super strict mom and the rockstar dreams?"

"Yep."

"That sounds just like me." Vee flashed her white teeth and giggled. "I love you, girl."

"I love you, too."

She rubbed my knee, her smile fading. "The bad news is ... Greyson is gone."

Frozen Whipped Cream Shapes

Recipe from Christene Houston

  Heavy whipping cream *DO NOT USE canned
    whipped cream*
  Sugar

In a mixer, whip a bowl of heavy whipping cream until stiff peaks form. Sweeten to taste with sugar.

Line a jelly roll pan with waxed paper. Spread whipped cream in a thick layer on the waxed paper. Top with sprinkles or other add-ins as desired. Freeze for 3 hours.

Using festive cookie cutters, cut out desired shapes.

Carefully remove from waxed paper and voilà! You have your shaped whipped cream for topping your cocoa. Freeze in a large ziplock with a layer of waxed paper in between each shape to keep them from sticking together.

CHAPTER ELEVEN

"Where is he?"

"He didn't say. He didn't tell anyone. He left the morning after you did. I kind of thought he might be coming after you, but …"

My head sank into my hands. "It's over then."

Vee clicked her tongue. "Have you even been listening to me? Where is your Rocky spirit? The Eye of the Tiger, girl. Go all Katy Perry on it, and hunt that puppy down!"

"How did you go from Sylvester Stallone to Katy Perry in one sentence? My head is spinning. Seriously, Vee."

"Stop critiquing my metaphors. Let's just face the facts that you have some hunting to do."

I rested back on the cushion, thinking. Mom said to live life with a capital L, to leave nothing on the table. If Greyson had gone, I needed to find him and somehow tell him how I felt, whether he wanted me or not. My fingers itched to call him, but the things I had to say couldn't be said over the phone or put down in a text. If he wasn't here, he would have gone home, to see his grandparents and Rosie. Somehow, I needed to find him before the sun set, before Christmas came and the magic disappeared.

"I know where he is."

"You do?"

"He grew up with his grandparents. I think he went home."

"Any ideas where that is?"

"Somewhere in the country, but that's all I've got." I looked at the ceiling for another long moment. "But I know who I could ask."

Vanessa Davenport was the perfect accomplice. She didn't mind spilling the beans about Greyson's possible whereabouts. She didn't mind me taking the SUV she loaned us in my pursuit of true love, as she put it. And she didn't mind that Vee would be flying solo on the sleigh ride outing we'd planned for this night, the night before Christmas.

It was a good two hours before I pulled into the driveway of a small house with a peaked roofline and tiny stoop. Snow covered the yard in a blanket of pristine white, but the pathway to the door was cleared and salted. I picked my way there, letting the act of not slipping occupy my mind over my fear of what I would say or do.

When I knocked, there was a long, cold silence before I heard rustling and then, finally, a woman opened the door. She was my height with white curls and softly rounded hips. "Can I help you?"

Blue eyes, almost the exact shade of Greyson's, made the connection crystal clear.

"Hi. I'm sorry to bother you on Christmas Eve. My name is Molly Hayes. I'm a friend of Greyson's. I … I wondered if he was here?"

Her look went from puzzled to pleasant. "Pleased to meet you, come in out of the cold. I just put on a pot of cocoa. You're welcome to have a cup."

"Thank you."

I stepped into a cozy little house, with arm chairs and a worn sofa in one room that we passed with barely a glance. Stepping into the kitchen, I knew this was where the real gathering took place. The table was small but inviting, the room smelled of chocolate, and the woman patted the counter where a row of barstools with hand-sewn cushions were tucked.

"Take a seat. You're looking for Greyson, you said?"

"Yes. I was hoping he might be here."

"He was." The old woman sighed as she ladled the co-coa from the pot on the cook top into mismatched mugs. One said "World's Best Grandma" in childish writing.

"But he didn't stay long. Came to make amends, visit Rosie's grave, and then he was off."

My heart sank to my toes. In the course of my travels, I hadn't let myself think of what I would do if he wasn't here.

I'm grateful for unexpected twists in my story.

"He … he left?"

"Said he had something to do." She nudged the cup into my hands, and I noticed a floating heart that was quickly disappearing in the hot brown liquid.

"What is this?"

"Whipped cream. I freeze a layer on the jelly roll pan and then cut them out in shapes. Used to do it for the kids, and now it's habit. Grandpa doesn't mind." She winked, and I noticed again how like Greyson's her eyes were.

"It's clever," I said, taking a sip and then looking up at her in surprise. "Is that cinnamon?"

"Mm-hmm." Her smile broadened. "I have some pumpkin cake over there if you'd like a little bite."

"That sounds delicious, Mrs. …"

"Janice Gregory."

"Mrs. Gregory, Greyson talked about your cooking. I should have known your cocoa would be phenomenal, too."

"My husband goes down to the fire station during the holidays to visit the boys. I make up a nice hot pot of cinnamon cocoa, frozen whipped cream, and lots of cookies for him to take with him. I'm glad Greyson thinks fondly on the forced labor of his childhood."

With a chuckle, I sipped my cocoa, trying to figure out where to go from here. I started to key in a text to him on my phone, but then erased it, nervous. Nervous that he wouldn't reply. Nervous he would. Just plain *nervous.*

"You know, I really thought he would be here. I'm not sure where else to look."

"You said your name is Molly?"

"Yes."

"He went looking for you." She brought the tray over with a slight shake in her hands and ran a knife through the pumpkin swirls, placing a thick square on a small cobalt plate before sliding it across the counter. She leaned in. "You may not know this, young lady, but you're something special."

My eyes widened. "Thank you."

"Don't look so surprised. Go ahead, give it a try."

I took the fork she offered and slid it through layers of streusel topping, pumpkin pie, and a cake batter crust. That first bite was a revelation of rich pumpkiny sweetness. "Mmm ... what did you say this was?"

"Pumpkin Cake." She grinned. "Family recipe."

"Is that a cake mix on the bottom? Wow, that is delicious."

Her blue eyes twinkled merrily as she took out a pencil and a scrap of paper. "Greyson said you were a baker. I knew you'd enjoy that."

"He talked about me?" I tried not to choke on my next bite. There was no reason to waste this kind of yumminess.

"You're *all* he talked about, after his apologies, mind you. We shed a lot of tears." She peered down at the paper while she wrote.

"I'm glad he came home. He missed you guys a lot."

She nodded, making another note. "He was a different man when he walked through that door. I think I have you to thank for that."

I shook my head. "Not me. I don't think I did much more than insult him and break his heart."

Mrs. Gregory made a clicking sound with her tongue. "How little we value the influence we have over our boys. Let me tell you something, Molly Hayes. I've known that boy since his mother dropped him on our doorstep at seven years old. He is a fighter. He and Rosie were cats and dogs during the early years, but when they reached their teens something special happened. They just clicked. Instead of annoying each other all the time, they were singing, going out to the river, and double dating.

As fierce as he was when they fought, he was even more loyal when they were friends. Her death was a low blow, one none of us saw coming. To this day we struggle to handle the absence of her bright spirit in our lives."

"I'm so sorry, Mrs. Gregory."

"I know you are dear. Loss makes you tender to the sorrow of others, doesn't it? I know it has me. Greyson mentioned your mother's passing. I'm sorry you lost her so young."

"Thank you." It was amazing to me that Greyson had shared so much about me in the short time he'd been home.

"When he left this house last Christmas, he was all fury and heartache. The young man who'd cheered his sister at her graduation and worked diligently in college was long gone, and there was nothing his grandpa or I could say to turn him around. There was no amount of understanding or talking that made him feel any better. What he wanted was to get away from it, to hide from the pain. But that's the trouble with this kind of ache, there's no hiding from it. It finds you on the sunniest day and pulls in the dark clouds. When you're laughing at a commercial, the next moment you can be in tears. You know. You've been there."

I nodded, solemnly. "It doesn't get easier. You just learn to bear it better."

Her brows lifted in surprise. "Yes. Exactly. My … that's a wise statement for one so young. Yes. You bear it. But he didn't want to bear it. He wanted relief. And that came from staying away, from trying to forget who he was. I told my husband he would come back in his own time, but it didn't hurt any less."

"We maintained a connection to the Davenports for the sake of the kids, though Mr. Davenport has led a rather selfish existence where it came to his children. With his money, he was generous, mind you. They never wanted for anything, and neither have we, for that matter, but we didn't tell the kids just how much he contributed every month." She chuckled. "Kids have to learn to work. We couldn't let them know they had thousands in the bank. When they learned to drive, it was on an old work truck. When they got their first cars they were junkers bought on sweat equity. When they finally found out they were rich, they were astounded. I think we got more than a few dirty looks over that one, especially from Rosie. She couldn't handle the memory of mucking stalls for prom money only to know she could have had any dress on the rack."

I couldn't help the smile that came with that image. "Man, that would be a harsh realization."

Mrs. Gregory just chuckled. "Well, like I said, last Christmas left us all more than a bit bereft. For Greyson especially, there was such a feeling of loss and failure to protect Rosie when that was his thing. I'm sure when you met him, he wasn't the kind of man you'd want to hang out with."

"No. We did not begin our relationship on pleasant terms."

"He was a pain in the butt, wasn't he?"

"Horrible."

"Mm-hmm, I assumed as much. What happened?"

I studied my cocoa, not sure how much to reveal. "He ended up on my doorstep."

"Was that the night he got drunk?"

I glanced up sharply. "How did you know?"

"He said something about not being himself one night. He's not a drinker. Never really got into that crowd, but more than once he's admitted to it when we spoke while he was away."

"Well, it was the only time I saw him that way if it gives you any comfort. I don't know what happened. One minute we were fighting, and the next—it was like he could see through me, and all my defenses were tossed aside. From that moment he was a different person. I started to see the Greyson I know now, someone thoughtful, tender and kind. Now I realize he wanted to do for me what he couldn't do for Rosie."

"He blamed himself," she said quietly. "He felt like he didn't do enough. We all did."

"He told me about her, and I somehow found a way to tell him about my mom. When I tell you sharing my story is a hard thing for me, that's an understatement. But I told him everything."

"And he still liked you." She seemed to know what I was thinking before I said the words. "You made a difference in him. I thank you for that. The man who returned to us is even better than the one we lost."

"I think I messed everything up," I said quietly, not daring to look into her lovely blue eyes.

"What happened?" She came around the counter and perched on the barstool beside me. It felt so much like we were old friends, already. Instead of giving in to my normal hesitation, I let it happen, turning to face her and tucking my hair behind one ear.

"I have some fear surrounding relationships. I mean … big fear. After losing Mom, I went through some major depression, and once I got through it I didn't think I could handle losing someone else that important in my life. Being with Greyson was the first time I've opened up to anyone. I don't know what he did, but suddenly we were together all the time. He would just show up and ask questions, and for some crazy reason, I would answer them. Three days ago, I got the call that my uncle was in the cardiac ICU after a heart attack. I just … I freaked out. I felt the darkness coming for me again, and it seemed like the universe was laughing at me. The thought of losing Frank was terrifying, and it cast everything else into shadow. When he asked to come with me, I pushed him away."

Mrs. Gregory sighed. "Doesn't it seem like the universe conspires against us? On our best days it can knock us flat on our faces with no warning. That was a real test of your newfound trust, and like most of us, you stumbled."

"Don't be nice, Mrs. Gregory. I biffed it, big time. Everything is okay. Frank is recovering. But I don't know if what Greyson and I had was strong enough to handle the mess that is Molly Hayes. I drove here with every intention of groveling."

Mrs. Gregory smiled. "Now, there's no need for that. You may have made a mistake, but a gentleman would never allow his lady to lose her self respect."

I looked at her quizzically. "I was horrible."

"Yes, but are any of us really innocent of being horrible at one time or another? I think you've got more going for you than you realize. He went after you."

"He did?"

"Didn't I mention that? He went back to the city to find you."

"But … but I'm not in the city!"

"I see that."

"So what do I do?"

"Well," Mrs. Gregory rose from the stool and walked a few paces, a thoughtful look on her face, "when I was a girl, a letter delivered by snail mail, as you youngsters call it, would have to suffice. But you have a lot of options, don't you?"

I nodded. "I'm so afraid he won't answer his phone."

"You'll never know if you don't make the call."

I pressed my lips together and stared at his number on my phone. Hearing his voice was just what I needed but feared the most. I wasn't ready to risk it, so instead I tapped out a message. Erased it. Tried another. Finally, I settled with: *This is Molly. I need to talk to you.*

Mrs. Gregory must have seen the anxiety on my face. She patted my hand and then whispered, "I'll just be in the other room if you need me." I watched her go, my heart beating in my ears, my hands shaking. Time seemed to warp and stretch, lengthening itself as my imagination ran wild with the possibilities. When the text came in, I jumped and suppressed a surprised squeal.

Where the heck are you?

I fought with autocorrect before I could send my reply.

At your Grandma's. There was a long pause before I added: *I was coming to apologize.*

Figures. I'm in the city. I didn't want to spook you by calling. Your uncle okay?

Recovering after emergency surgery. He's doing well.

Glad to hear it.

I sighed, staring out the window for a long moment before writing: *What would Scrooge do?*

Besides crashing his employee's family dinner?

I laughed out loud before replying: *He did bring the roasted bird.*

Doesn't make it any less creepy.

What would he do, I wondered? Scrooge, who knew how to keep Christmas better than any other? And then it struck me. Of course. He would find a way to be together.

Meet me at the inn?

Already on my way. Can I get another ticket to the Ice Capades?

I'll save my best spins for you.

Be safe. We have a lot to talk about.

I sighed. Despite the silly banter, a feeling of dread filled my heart as I said my goodbyes to Mrs. Gregory.

"Don't forget this." She held up the note she'd written. In fine cursive was the recipe for her Pumpkin Cake.

"You're sharing your cake recipe?"

"Why not? With any luck, we'll end up keeping it in the family!"

* * *

If two hours seemed like a lifetime on the drive down, the return trip felt millennial. My brain kept up a running tab of why Greyson should refuse my apologies and even the festive music on the radio didn't lift my spirits.

It was only in the end, when *It Came Upon A Midnight Clear* came over the speakers that I wiped away my last tears and took comfort in this thought: maybe my Scroogey life wouldn't end wrapped up in a sweet red bow on Christmas morning. But just like him, I was different now. Different forever. Greyson may not forgive me, but that wouldn't stop me from opening my heart when the next opportunity came along. It wouldn't keep me from living my life with a capital L.

Driving into the parking lot at the inn, I wasn't surprised to see his SUV already parked there. I whispered a prayer and a list of gratitude's before opening the door.

I'm grateful for Christmas Eve, when miracles are most potent.

I'm grateful for a letter from my mother when I needed it most.

I'm grateful Greyson's grandma was so nice.

I'm grateful for pumpkin cake and frozen whipped cream.

I'm grateful to believe I am worth loving.

I was in the middle of that last one when there was a tap on my window. Of all the people I'd expected to see,

Big Ben's white bearded face was not one of them. I opened the door in surprise.

"Hey, Ben." I grabbed my bag and slid out onto the snow covered parking lot.

"Hi, Miss Molly. Greyson sent me out to getcha. How's you're uncle?"

I tipped my head back to reply. "Double bypass, but recovering well. Thanks for asking."

A silence followed where I was too busy battling the butterflies in my stomach to move. Finally, I squared my shoulders, determined to face the situation head on.

"Don't mean to interrupt ya, but had you thought on turning out those lights?"

I whirled and, sure enough, my lights were still glowing in the feeble afternoon light. With a groan, I reached back in and flipped the switch. I guess I was never going to learn that lesson. Sheesh!

Turning back toward the walk, I started forward.

"We're headin' this way," Ben interrupted again, pointing to the other end of the parking lot. There, standing in the snow, was a beautiful horse breathing smoke into the chill air. He was hitched with a jingle bell harness that shifted musically when he pawed at the ground. Behind him was a sleigh, the one we'd rented for tonight's festivities, edged in more bells.

"You want me to get in that?" It wasn't how I'd pictured this whole thing going down.

"It's the sleigh, or if you're feelin' adventurous, we could resort to snowshoes. Though I reckon it'll take a bit longer to get to where Greyson's waitin'." Ben stroked his long beard thoughtfully.

"On another day, I might take you up on the snowshoes, but this isn't one of those days. Let's go with the sleigh."

"Good choice," Ben chuckled, offering his arm. At the sleigh he handed me in and then pointed out a jacket and blanket for tucking in around my legs.

"Sun'll be settin' here soon. You'll want to hunker down a bit and let Hudson take us up and over the hill." He stepped up into the seat, taking the reins in hand.

"I'm in your hands," I told him, snuggling down under the comforter and pulling mittens from the pockets of my jacket.

"Then you'll be just fine. Gidd'up!"

There was something magical about gliding over the snow, jingle bells prancing with each raise of the horse's hooves. In the midst of the magic, the reality of what was to come sank into my heart with the gathering cold. Deep inside, I had to come to terms with the facts of the matter. There were things I needed to say to Greyson, and this could be the last time I'd get the chance. I wanted our story to end just like the Christmas Carol of old—with redemption and hopes for the future. But I didn't know if reality would match up with fiction.

Soon we were up and over a hill, down through a valley, and up again, approaching a beautiful stream that still gurgled hopefully beneath a growing layer of ice. At the top of the rise stood a bridge that stretched itself across the expanse of the stream. My heart skipped a beat when I spotted Greyson's figure at its center, hunched down in his coat against the cold, ski cap pulled low over his brows.

Hudson pulled us to a stop at one end of the bridge, and Ben handed me down.

"What is this place, Ben?"

"Angel Bridge. Many a miracle has happened on this here bridge." He turned to go back toward the sleigh. "Good luck, Molly. You can speak up, if you like, so I have some gossip to share back down the hill." He chuckled as he walked back to Hudson, patting his neck and feeding him something from his pocket.

I faced Greyson just as he turned my way, his eyes capturing mine. There was a moment of silence, bursting with anticipation, fear, and the unknown. I couldn't hold back any longer, and a sudden sob filled my chest. "Greyson."

He opened his arms. "Come 'ere."

I walked, and then jogged, flinging my arms around him. With my lips against his neck I whispered, "I'm so sorry, Greyson. I was so wrong to run away like that."

He pulled back a little, looking down into my face. "That kind of fear doesn't just go away, you know?"

"I know." I had so much to say. I wanted to unlock my heart and lay it at his feet, but he stopped me.

"I've been thinking a lot, Molly. Driving gives you a lot of time with your thoughts, you know? I've been … wondering. Wondering if I'm walking into another Rosie situation. Am I trying to rescue someone who's not ready to be saved?" His smile was sad. "You know how God seems to keep showing you the same lesson until you get it right?"

"Greyson …"

I felt a tear trickle down my cheek, a weight of sorrow settling down on my shoulders. I was losing him.

"Let me say this, okay? It's hard for me and I don't want to lose my nerve." He said as he pulled away, walking to the bridge railing and looking down at the frozen water below. "Thank you for what you said. I appreciate knowing that after how we left things. And thank you for coming here, for letting me have this closure that I need. With Rosie, there was nothing, and it hurts every day knowing I didn't say what needed to be said. I missed my chance with her. That's one thing I swore I would never do again, and yet I almost let it happen. The morning you left, I kicked myself thinking that I should never have let you go without me."

I had so much to say, but I honored his wishes and watched him from where he'd left me, taking every facet of him into my memory. The way his beard had grown in thicker since I left, and the way his brow furrowed as he spoke, making his eyes sad.

"I went home, but you know that now. It was you who helped me have the courage, to know that the life I was living wasn't one I could be proud of. You were my ghosts, Molly. Past, present," he paused, looking at me for a long moment, "and future. You helped me see what I was missing out on by not facing my loss. I'll be forever grateful for that.

"There's nothing like a 2 am call to show you who you really are. I'll never forget how it changed me with Rosie, and it changed me with you. When that door closed behind you, I knew I had to figure it out. Was I going to relive my fears over and over? Was I going to stand there waiting for the next disaster that would leave me feeling like a failure? For two years I've been running from the fact that I didn't do enough for my sister. I've let it haunt me and run me ragged. I've been a shadow of myself and I've sacrificed the things and people I love because I thought ... I thought it was my fault. I know you didn't mean to, but when you left, those old feelings came flooding back. I wondered if there would ever be a time I could be enough. If I could love enough, give enough, be strong enough for the people I care about."

I swiped at the tears on my cheeks. My heart was breaking. I knew I'd hurt Greyson, but I hadn't thought of how my leaving would rip open his tender wounds. It made his desire to end things with me a more obvious choice. Of course he would. I was so wrapped up in myself, in my own misery, even now. He needed someone who could love him without all this mess in the way.

"When I went home, my grandma accepted all my apologies, like it had never happened. Over a year of pushing her away, only calling when I had to, ignoring the phone when I saw her name on it and she acted like it was nothing. Like having me in her life was worth every sacrifice along the way." He swiped at a tear and held up his hands. "Who does that?"

I could only smile sadly. Opening my mouth would produce a sob, and I didn't want to embarrass myself just yet. He walked to me and took my hands in his, staring at them as he spoke.

"I asked her how she could do it. And she said, 'When you love someone, you love them, thorns and roses.' She said she'd learned through her life of choices to forgive and forget quickly, because you never know how many minutes are left with the people who mean the most. Talking to her, that's when I got it. I don't have to rescue anyone. You don't need me to save you from the heartache of your past or your fears of the future. And I am enough if I let myself just love—in spite of all the reasons not to. The answer to all of this is love.

"Love is enough for when we hurt each other, when we let go instead of holding on tight, when we forget who we are and how much we need each other. Love is what Scrooge found that night so long ago, on the cusp of being too late. He realized that living a life without love was not living at all; it wasn't even existing. It's worse; it's hiding from life. Love is the key."

I stared at our hands, too heartbroken to look into his face when he said the final words.

"I love you, Molly."

My head snapped up. "What?"

"I love you. If you don't remember anything else that I said here tonight, remember I love you. That's all I have to say."

I stood there, mouth gaping open, my head spinning.

"You ... love me? But Greyson, so much of me is broken, jumbled drama."

"And I love you," he repeated, stepping closer, pressing his hand against my cheek. "I love the messy, broken drama queen that is you, Molly Hayes."

I was crying harder now, tears flooding my cheeks as the truth rang through me. This was the dream I'd been hoping for before I knew it was possible. Greyson loved me, not because I had it all together, but in spite of the missing parts, the mistakes, the weaknesses that were part of who I was.

Greyson used the pad of his glove to wipe the tears from my cheek. "You're kinda leavin' me hanging here. This would be a great time for you to say something."

I slid my arms up around his neck and pressed my forehead to his for a long moment, trying to get my emotions under control. When I lifted my head, I could finally form the words that had been beating in my heart for so long now.

"I woke up this morning with the sole goal of finding you and telling you how very sorry I was. I was so foolish to run off and push you away in the process. I had no idea I made you feel that way and it breaks my heart." I paused, overwhelmed by the emotion that swelled in my chest. Tears gathered on my lashes and dripped onto my cheeks and I wiped them away with my sleeve. "I could only think of what I was losing and what it would mean if *you* were in that hospital. You're right when you say that kind of fear doesn't just go away. It's something that I'll live with every single day of my life. But I'm learning. I'm learning that there's no way to live without loving people. I'm learning that to honor my mother I can't hide my heart away. I have to be willing to take risks and allow someone into my life.

"Greyson, I am broken. That brokenness has opened my heart and left a space. At first I thought there was no way to fill it, no way to compensate for the void that was created. I kept that space vacant to honor a memory and protect myself. Now I know it was made to be filled. Like that wonderful Christmas story, I want to love so that people will say I knew how to do it best. I want to live in capital letters. I want to love when it's easy, when it's not, when it's fun, and when it's the hardest choice I'll ever make. My life is not complete without letting someone fill in the broken places. Greyson, I want that someone to be you."

He shook his head in disbelief. "Are you serious?"

I smacked my hand against his chest. "What did you think I was rushing here to tell you?"

"I thought you were coming to tell me it wasn't going to work. That after this scare with your uncle you were more sure than ever that you needed to be alone."

The look in his eyes made my heart still. I realized that despite his own fears he'd been strong enough to confront them, to bare his heart even when there was no guarantee. I was in love with the bravest man I knew. And more than ever, I wanted to love him, shelter him and bear what life threw at us, together.

"Greyson, I love you, and I want to take this risk. With you." I pressed my lips to his and repeated the words with every breath. "I love you, I love you, I love you."

It was a long moment before he pulled back, pressing his forehead against mine. "I think today is living proof that Christmas miracles really happen."

I grinned. "And on that happy note, I must confess I may lose a butt cheek to hypothermia if we stay out here any longer."

He laughed outright. "Now that would be a crying shame. Let's go."

Pulling me in tight to his side, we walked to the sleigh where Ben and Hudson were waiting. Greyson shook hands with Ben.

"Thanks for waiting, Ben. We had a lot to say." Greyson helped me into the sleigh and sat down beside me.

"Happy to. Though I dare say Hudson likes to be movin' in this cold."

The sleigh jumped to life as Hudson pulled us back over the snow to the inn with bells filling the air. We huddled down under the blanket, our foreheads together, lips often touching, promises spoken while starlight filled the night sky.

Emogene's Pumpkin Cake

Recipe from Emogene Houston

  1 box yellow cake mix
  3/4 c. butter, divided
  4 eggs
  1 lb. or 2 c. canned pumpkin
  1 1/2 tsp. cinnamon
  1/2 c. brown sugar
  1 (6 oz.) can evaporated milk
  1/2 c. white sugar

Preheat oven to 350° F. Set aside one cup of cake mix.

For the first layer, mix the remaining cake mix with 1/2 cup butter and one egg. Press into bottom of 9 x 13 in. greased pan.

For the next layer, combine pumpkin, three remaining eggs, brown sugar, cinnamon, and milk. Mix until blended. Spread over crust.

For the crumb topping, combine 1/4 cup soft butter, white sugar, and reserved cup of cake mix. Sprinkle over pumpkin. Using a knife, swirl crumb mixture throughout pumpkin mixture without disturbing bottom layer of crust.

Bake at 350° F for 45-60 minutes. Bake until a knife inserted in the center comes out clean.

EPILOGUE

That Christmas Day was a Norman Rockwell painting of perfection. Family around the table at the inn, Christmas lights twinkling in the background, a sumptuous breakfast casserole, and fried bread smothered in honey and butter to tempt us away from the chaos of torn wrapping paper and new toys at brunch time.

Greyson and I were too busy driving past each other the day before to have time to shop for just the right thing. Instead, we spent the morning sketching out a new design with my updated shop name, Cookie Girl, front and center. Despite all my protests, that darn nickname had really grown on me. And now, when he whispered it in my ear, it sent shivers down my neck and across my shoulders.

While we brainstormed ideas about the shop and our future together, Vee was busy talking about her wedding plans with Lucille and Ben—who just happened to be an ordained minister.

Weddings would be the subject of choice for the next six months. And, true to her word, Vee's summer wedding at the inn was gorgeous. Classic elegance abounded with rich purple and touches of gold. The cookies, courtesy of Cookie Girl Bakery, were a scalloped circle with Vee and Jon's monogram in their colors atop a flood of cream. There were rose petals and candles in cream, accented everywhere by purple flowers. There were cake pops—with gold and purple edible beads—and special made cookie favors wrapped in gauzy gold bags to take home.

All that glorious perfection helped make up for the fact that Greyson and I sported platinum rings before Jon and Vee did.

Late in the spring, before the snow melted completely, he took me to see my mother and then asked on one knee. There was no other response than "yes." We made it official in a quiet ceremony with Vee and Jon, Karen and Frank, and the kids, as well as Greyson's family with Grandma and Grandpa Gregory. I wore a dress with a dreamy high waistline and flowing fabric. He wore a tux that made him look sinfully handsome.

The ceremony took place on a bridge not far from the inn, a bridge that spanned an expanse of rushing, gurgling water. Shoeless in the springtime sun, my toes sparkled in robin's egg blue, and the cuffs of his pants were rolled. Around my neck was my mother's necklace, one she wore on her wedding day. Greyson wore his sister's class ring on his pinkie finger. Both of us felt sure Rosie and mom were in attendance on that happy day.

As the sun set, we vowed to love each other through darkness and sun, through happiness and misery. We promised to rescue each other every day, and to be grateful. Grateful for sunshine after a storm. Grateful for friends who don't go away even when you tell them to. Grateful for heartaches, because they brought us together one snowy Christmas. And grateful for bridges over sorrow, leading to a happiness that would be strong enough to weather the troubles of tomorrow.

Greyson Davenport lifted my veil while Karen wiped away tears at one end of the bridge and Vee beamed at me from beside Ben. When the final words were said, Greyson stepped in close and kissed me. It wasn't short and sweet. Oh no. He put his arms around me, pulling me in so that my thighs touched his. He traced one finger down my cheek like he had that night so long ago and smiled that terrible, cocky smirk he wore so well.

"You tried to run away from me once, Molly. But somehow, we found each other again. I hope you know I intend to spend the rest of my life making your dreams come true, my spirited, talented, beautiful Cookie Girl." And with that, he pressed his lips to mine. I would always remember the way he felt in my arms, the amazing smell of his cologne that filled my senses, and my fingertips brushing the edge of his hairline. It was a crazy, irrational risk, this loving a man like I loved Greyson Davenport. But hey, that's what Living is all about.

THE END

The Twelve Parties of Christmas

First Day of Christmas: Kick off the Season Dinner Party

Second Day of Christmas: Trim the Tree

Third Day of Christmas: Ice Skating and Hot Cocoa Bar

Fourth Day of Christmas: Nutcracker Party

Fifth Day of Christmas: Cookie Exchange

Sixth Day of Christmas: Gingerbread House Party

Seventh Day of Christmas: Movie Night

Eighth Day of Christmas: Reindeer Games

Ninth Day of Christmas: Christmas Stories

Tenth Day of Christmas: Formal Dinner Party

Eleventh Day of Christmas: Nativity Reenactment

Twelfth Day of Christmas: Caroling Sleigh Ride

For games, menu ideas and recipes, visit my blog at: Christenehouston.com/blog and my Snowflake Falls Inn Romance Pinterest board: pinterest.com/christeneh/a-snow flake-falls-inn-romance/

ACKNOWLEDGMENTS

Molly spends a lot of time thinking about what she's grateful for. I want to spend some time doing the same. I am grateful for my Heavenly Father who has blessed me with talents and given me courage to follow them. If the words I write inspire, bring joy or laughter or lift any human soul, it is because of the goodness of God and all praise and honor can go directly back to that source.

Without the optimism and support of my husband Kevin and my five remarkably busy and fabulous kids, I know this book would never have happened. I want to thank them for enduring a house that's messier than normal and dinners that come out of a box or drive thru more often than they should. Thank you for asking questions and showing interest. A special thanks to my husband for listening to me debate the merits of one scene or another during date nights. His unfailing belief that I know what I'm doing has helped me weather many a dark moment. I especially appreciate his cool head when things got crazy during the final hours with corrupted documents and panicky phone calls. To my children, I must say, being a mother to them in all it's carpooling, homework checking, diaper changing glory is still one of my very favorite things to do.

A huge thanks to Emily for her tireless help in editing, cleaning up my grammar errors and bearing my writing quirks with patience and cheer. Your talents are valuable and I am grateful that you put them to work in my behalf. This book is better because of your hard work. Thank you, thank you!

Because Molly is a baker, I could not write her story without delicious recipes to go along with it. Thank you to Janeen, Jamie and Amber for their generous donation of delicious, time tested recipes. They are the fancy sprinkles on top of this cookie.

Many sincere thanks to those who were my beta readers and offered their kind input and took of their time to perfect this book. Angie, Kim, Katie, and Ruth, thank you so much for your support. You're kindness and gentle guidance are so appreciated. There is something so wonderful about being surrounded by talented, beautiful and genuine people. I adore each one of you. Thank you for being my friends through sunshine and rain.

Most writers love books and the same is true for me. I appreciate my book club, the Chapter Chicks who are a constant source of inspiration and support. What would I do without these ladies in my life? Thank you for being your witty, remarkable selves!

Thank you, most sincerely, to my readers. To every friend who has stopped to ask me when my next book comes out or written a review or told a friend when they asked for a good book to read. I adore you! Your kind words lift my soul and banish my doubts. They give me courage to write when the words don't always come easily. I can't begin to tell you what your simple but profound kindness does to make the world a better place.

This book touches on a few tender subjects. One is cancer. My husband lost his sweet mother Emogene to cancer while still in his teens. Since we wed fourteen years ago, there have been countless moments when I have longed to have this special woman in my life and the lives of my little ones. She was my inspiration for Molly's mom in many ways. The way she treasured Christmas was beautiful to behold, and we've all benefited from her example of love. While she has not been with us here on earth, I have felt her loving care over us and especially for my children. Thank you Gene.

I want to extend another very tender thanks to those I know who have struggled with depression. Thank you for sharing your hearts with me. Every story, experience and heartache has shaped my heart and given me understanding I didn't know I needed. I honor you for your strength.

If you have dreamed of being a writer, there is no better time than now to begin your pursuit. Our days are not limitless, but your potential is. If you're not sure where to start, let me recommend the LDS Storymakers Conference. You will meet talented and friendly people with minds that work like yours in many ways and yet find unique expression. You will be able to hone your skills and grow your courage. Check it out.

To all those who inspire me in their everyday walk of life, thank you. I am grateful for you.

For more information about my books and writing, follow me on FB (Christene Houston, Author), on Twitter @WriterChristene, on my blog Christenehouston.com and Pinterest (Christene Houston). My first book, A Heart So Broken, can also be found on Amazon.com. If you are interested in having me visit your book club or school, drop me a line at Christenehouston@aol.com.

Cookie Girl Christmas is part of the Snowflake Falls Inn Romance collection. Be watching for book two out in Summer 2015.

Made in the USA
San Bernardino, CA
24 May 2018